WORSE THAN A BULLET IN THE BACK

Skye Fargo wasn't one to shoot a man in the back —even a bloodthirsty Cheyenne. He whispered, "Hey!", so the brave would wheel and face him. Then Skye's Sharps spoke—blasting the Cheyenne away.

Suddenly iron arms encircled him from behind. He was lifted bodily and shaken violently. The Sharps flew from his hand and he was flung facedown into the cold Kansas snow. A heavy body was on his back, clinging to him like a snapping turtle.

Skye winced when his head was pulled sharply upward. He knew what his foe wanted to do. Snap his spinal cord like a toothpick. Each second brought his head farther back, closer to agonizing death . . . unless Skye figured out incredibly fast how to do the impossible. . . .

THE TRAILSMAN

125

BLOOD PRAIRIE

by

Jon Sharpe

A SIGNET BOOK

SIGNET
Published by the Penguin Group
Penguin Books USA Inc., 375 Hudson Street,
New York, New York, 10014, U.S.A.
Penguin Books Ltd, 27 Wrights Lane, London W8 5TZ, England
Penguin Books Australia Ltd, Ringwood, Victoria, Australia
Penguin Books Canada Ltd, 10 Alcorn Avenue, Toronto, Ontario M4V 3B2
Penguin Books (N.Z.) Ltd, 182-190 Wairau Road,
Auckland 10, New Zealand

Penguin Books Ltd, Registered Offices:
Harmondsworth, Middlesex, England

First published by Signet, an imprint of New American Library,
a division of Penguin Books USA Inc.

First Printing, May, 1992

10 9 8 7 6 5 4 3 2 1

The first chapter of this book originally appeared in *Colorado Quarry*,
the one hundred twenty-fourth volume in this series.

 REGISTERED TRADEMARK—MARCA REGISTRADA

PRINTED IN THE UNITED STATES OF AMERICA

The Trailsman

Beginnings . . . they bend the tree and they mark the man. Skye Fargo was born when he was eighteen. Terror was his midwife, vengeance his first cry. Killing spawned Skye Fargo, ruthless, cold-blooded murder. Out of the acrid smoke of gunpowder still hanging in the air, he rose, cried out a promise never forgotten.

The Trailsman they began to call him all across the West: searcher, scout, hunter, the man who could see where others only looked, his skills for hire but not his soul, the man who lived each day to the fullest, yet trailed each tomorrow. Skye Fargo, the Trailsman, the seeker who could take the wildness of a land and the wanting of a woman and make them his own.

*1860—on the long, hard trail
between the Territory of Kansas and
the booming town of Denver,
a trail littered with the bones
of those who died along the way.*

1

The blizzard swept out of the west with all the fury of a rampaging grizzly bear.

An hour before, the big man had been riding westward across the plains of Kansas at an easygoing pace, his magnificent Ovaro stallion covering the miles effortlessly. The superbly muscled forms of both the rider and the horse flowed together in perfect coordination. Here was a man born to the saddle and a horse with all the spirit and stamina of a wild mustang. They were part and parcel of the endless tract of grassland surrounding them, as at home on the plains as the buffalo and the coyote.

The big man's penetrating lake-blue eyes had narrowed when the roiling bank of slate-gray clouds first appeared on the horizon and came directly toward him. He'd straightened, inhaling the crisp, cool air deeply, and shifted to survey the grassland on both sides. Nowhere was there a place to take shelter, not even so much as a sparse stand of trees, and he'd urged the stallion to go faster.

Now, an hour later, he still sought a spot to sit out the inevitable storm. A lifetime spent in the wild enabled him to read the weather like most men could read a book, and he knew the recent snap of unseasonably mild January weather was about to take a dramatic turn for the worse. By next morning the plains would likely be buried under a foot or more of snow.

The prospect of heavy snow didn't worry him. He'd lived through snowstorms before and would do so again. His saddlebags contained plenty of jerked beef, coffee, and other victuals, so he wouldn't starve should game prove difficult to obtain. More worrisome was the drop in temperature. Already the temperature must have plunged ten degrees, and by nightfall it would undoubtedly hover near zero or below.

Skye Fargo glanced up at the thick blanket of clouds blotting out the entire sky and frowned. Soon the flurries would commence and he had yet to find a place to hole up in. He was scores of miles from the nearest settlement and the closest fort lay hundreds of miles away. There might be an Indian village in the general vicinity but, if so, it was probably Cheyenne and some of the young bucks had been kicking up their heels lately, waylaying unwary travelers. He wouldn't feel very safe staying with them.

Unfortunately, the grasslands of Kansas were as flat as a plate. Not without reason had they once been widely known as the Great American Desert. Adequate natural shelters were few and far between. Much farther west, along the foothills of the Rockies, and back east in the forested tracts of Missouri, there were plenty of places to take shelter from the elements. Not so in Kansas—unless a man could burrow into the ground like a prairie dog.

Ten minutes later the snow began. Initially the few flakes were small and fluttered to the earth in the stiff breeze. Gradually the size of the flakes increased and the trickle became a downpour.

Fargo twisted to untie the heavy sheepskin coat rolled up behind his saddle along with his bedroll. Donning the coat, he flipped the collar erect to keep the flakes from his neck, but he left the front of the coat unbuttoned to give him quick access to the Colt .44 strapped to his right hip. In addition to the revolver, he had a Sharps rifle snug in its saddle holster and a razor-sharp throwing knife—his Arkansaw toothpick—in a sheath in his right boot. He was exceptionally adept with all three weapons and felt confident he could handle any trouble that came his way.

The snow whispered as it fell, a soft sigh much like that of a woman in a passionate embrace. Soon a thin white layer covered the ground and more piled on top with every passing second.

Fargo felt the wind pick up. Visibility was now restricted to under twenty yards, which made it difficult for him to spot a resting place. Having no other recourse, he forged onward, his shoulders hunched against the biting cold. The Ovaro's hoofs thudded dully on the ground, its breath issuing from its nostrils in smoky puffs.

In no time at all the plains had been transformed into a winter wonderland. The snow depth rose from an inch to two inches, then to three.

Fargo couldn't take his bearings by the sun and had no landmarks to rely upon. He counted on his unerring instincts to take him in the right direction. If a man lived in the wilderness long enough, he sometimes acquired the ability to figure out which way was which by relying on a sort of sixth sense, on a mysterious inner compass as reliable as any ever made. Many Indians had the knack, as did the old-timer mountain men, and every scout worthy of the name had it too.

As one of the generally acknowledged top scouts in the West, Fargo seldom became lost. Even when in totally unfamiliar country, he invariably found his way around with an ease born of long experience. And it was safe to say that few living men had covered as much territory as he had. Kit Carson was one. The legendary Jim Bridger was another notable exception. Like them, he was a wanderer who couldn't abide staying in any one place very long. If he wasn't on the go, he wasn't happy.

Now though, Skye Fargo found himself wistfully wishing he'd stayed in Kansas City with Eleanor for a few more days. Cuddling with her warm, voluptuous body sure beat freezing his ass off in a blinding snowstorm any day of the week. Thinking of the way she had liked to sit astride him, bucking in pleasure until she was totally spent, brought a smile to his lips. She had been all woman.

The snowfall intensified, and Fargo could feel the cold flakes sticking to his face and throat. He pulled his hat down tighter around his ears and his coat collar up higher. Tucking his chin to his chest, he rode ever westward. Time lost all meaning. He was aware of the plodding Ovaro and the falling snow and nothing else.

Much later, when he estimated sunset couldn't be more than an hour off and he had about resigned himself to making camp on the open prairie, he came on the tracks. Surprised, he drew rein and stared down at the freshly made wagon-wheel marks, unable to explain their presence.

Fargo, as was his habit, was well off the beaten path. Ten miles or more to his north was the rutted trail used by the majority of pilgrims heading through the Kansas Territory to the gold fields in the Rockies. Anyone traveling westward in a wagon would be bound to use that trail, if only because there were a few way stations along the route where a body could feed stock, rest, and enjoy a hot meal.

But right there, inches from the pinto's front legs, were the distinct tracks left by a number of wagons making to the southwest. Fargo leaned down to examine them closely. The edges were still clear, the bottom of the ruts hardly covered with snow, which indicated the wagons had passed this way a very short time ago. Straightening, he gazed into the storm in the direction the wagons had gone. Where the hell were they going? he reflected. There was nothing out there except mile after mile of prairie. No towns. No settlements. No ranches or farms or anything.

It didn't make sense.

Fargo went to spur the Ovaro westward, then hesitated. What if those people were lost? What if they'd somehow strayed from the trail, then became disoriented in the storm? He figured there were six or seven wagons, judging from the tracks. There might be women and children on board. And since the storm had worsened to where it was almost a blizzard, those folks might find themselves in a lot of trouble come morning. He could be of help. But should he bother? After all, there might be a logical reason for the wagons being so far off the beaten track. Going after them could turn out to be a waste of time better spent seeking shelter from the snowstorm.

What should he do?

Fargo stared westward, then down at the wagon tracks. If there was one lesson every man who lived in the West learned sooner or later, it was never to meddle in the affairs of others. Sticking your nose in where it didn't belong could be downright dangerous. On the other hand, it was natural for strangers to offer a helping hand to anyone in need. That thought caused him to spur the Ovaro along the trail. He stayed to the left of the ruts, riding hard, eager to get it over with and be on his way if it should develop that he was on a fool's errand. Since he wasn't far behind the wagon, he'd overtake them in five or ten minutes.

The snow fell faster. The wind began to howl and whipped the flakes against his exposed skin, stinging him with tiny spears of fleeting pain. The cold worsened.

Fargo breathed shallowly to keep the searing cold out of his lungs. His nostrils tingled in the frigid air. He longed for a roaring fire to get his blood flowing again and a steaming cup of coffee to warm his insides. The tracks, thankfully, continued to be easy to read, the edges sharply defined, leading him to speculate that he was rapidly gaining ground. Moments later, in confirmation, a horse whinnied somewhere up ahead.

Skye squinted into the storm, seeking the wagons, and spied a large, vague shape at the limits of his vision. Slowing, he cupped his right hand to his mouth, about to call out and let them know he was friendly. The last thing he wanted was a nervous greenhorn taking a potshot at him. Suddenly, to his right, someone shrieked a single word.

"Indians!"

A gun boomed, and Fargo felt the slug tug at his hat. He shifted in the saddle, his right hand streaking toward his Colt, aware he was already too late. A lean figure launched itself from out of the white shroud and sinewy arms looped around his waist. The impact knocked him off the Ovaro, his attacker clinging to him as they fell.

Somewhere, there were loud shouts.

Landing hard on his right side, Fargo winced in pain. A fist slammed into his stomach but the blow, lacking strength, barely fazed him. He placed both hands on the shoulders of his attacker and shoved, tearing the man off and getting a good look at his face. That's when he discovered it wasn't a man. His attacker was a youth of fifteen or sixteen, no older.

"Indians!" the youth screamed. "Indians!"

Fargo saw the youth's eyes alight on his face, saw the shock of recognition as the tenderfoot realized he wasn't a red man after all, and then he delivered a punch of his own to the teenager's midsection, doubling the youth over. "I'm no Indian, you idiot," he snapped.

The youth gurgled and sputtered, his hat falling off as he thrashed his head from side to side. His face turned beet-red.

Running feet pounded. Shadowy forms converged, attended by loud yells.

"What the hell is going on?"

"Where are the Indians?"

"Over this way!"

"It's the Tyler kid!"

Fargo stood, brushing snow off his clothes, and swung around to face the newcomers, who collectively drew up short in consternation. There were eight, all told, with more coming. The youth rose slowly to his knees and grabbed his fallen hat.

"Who are you, mister?" demanded a burly man in a fur-collared coat and a derby. In his right hand was a Smith and Wesson that he leveled at Fargo's gut.

"I don't like having hoglegs pointed my way," Skye said. "Put that away before I make you eat it."

"Now see here," chimed in a blond man wearing fancy store-bought duds. "We don't know who you are and we have no reason to trust you. For all we know, you might have been sneaking up on us to rob us."

"Yeah," added another man belligerently. "Why else did you beat up the kid there?"

"I'm not a kid!" Tyler exploded angrily, rising with his fists clenched. "And I'll pound the next one who says I am."

For a second all eyes were on the youth, and Fargo instantly used the distraction to take a quick stride and swat the Smith and Wesson aside while simultaneously drawing his Colt and ramming the barrel into the burly man's abdomen. "I told you to put your hardware away," he growled, and cocked the Colt's hammer so everyone could hear it click. "I won't tell you again."

The burly man looked into Fargo's eyes and gulped. A strained silence descended as everyone froze. They were all apprehensive, fearing the gunshot they certainly believed would shatter the stillness.

"Hold on there, handsome," said a calm female voice in a decidedly friendly tone. "Pete is just looking out for our interests, that's all. He doesn't mean any harm. Why, he's never shot so much as a rabbit."

Fargo glanced at the speaker, a shapely redhead in a gray

dress and a black shawl, who was pressing through the group. "Pete doesn't listen very well," he commented, and reached out to pluck the Smith and Wesson from the man's unresisting fingers. Stepping back, he holstered the Colt and wedged the Smith and Wesson under his belt.

"Apparently we've gotten off on the wrong foot," the woman said, stopping right in front of Fargo. She fearlessly studied his features, her own showing intense curiosity.

"You can say that again," Fargo said. "I came on your tracks a while back and figured I'd check to see if you folks needed help. The next thing I know, someone tries to blow my head off and Tyler here jumps me."

The redhead turned to the youth. "I thought I heard you shouting something about Indians."

Tyler frowned and averted his gaze. "I was keeping watch like Briggs wanted when I saw a horse and rider come out of nowhere. The snow's so thick I couldn't see all that well." He nodded at Fargo. "All I saw was buckskins, so I thought it must be Indians."

"Was that you who fired?" the redhead inquired.

"Yep. Snapped off a shot without thinking," Tyler said sheepishly. "I'm really sorry, Molly."

"Don't tell me," Molly responded, and gestured at Skye. "He's the one you should be apologizing to."

"Sorry, mister."

Fargo's anger subsided. He couldn't stay mad at a green kid and a bunch of pilgrims who didn't have enough sense to find shelter out of the storm. "A man should always know what he's shooting at before he squeezes a trigger," he admonished the youth.

"It won't happen again," Tyler said.

"Where's your rifle?" Molly asked.

"I dropped it when I jumped the stranger," Tyler explained. "I knew I wouldn't have time to reload before he got off a shot, so I up and tackled him." He pivoted. "I'd better find that gun before the snow covers it." Off he went.

"My name is Molly Howard," the redhead said, and offered her right hand. "Who are you?"

"Skye Fargo," he answered, gently taking her palm in his.

Her hand was shapely and her grip surprisingly firm. He noticed the way her bosom made the shawl swell outward and her attractively slim hips. "Pleased to make your acquaintance."

The man called Pete coughed. "We're getting set to pitch camp for the night, Mr. Fargo. You're welcome to join us if you want. I'm sure Buffalo Briggs won't mind."

"You're fixing to make camp here?" Fargo asked.

"Close by," Pete said. "Buffalo Briggs says the storm will blow over in a couple of hours and we can resume our journey."

"Who is this Buffalo Briggs you keep talking about?"

"He's our wagon master."

From behind the onlookers, who now numbered sixteen people, came a stern voice. "Let me through, folks." The group parted to permit a tall, lanky man attired in buckskins and a fringed buckskin coat to advance. He wore a high white hat, a flowing red bandana, and white gloves. Strapped around his waist, outside the coat, were two nickel-plated, ivory-handled Colts. A flowing mustache and a neatly trimmed beard decorated his haughty face. "I'm George Briggs, but everyone calls me Buffalo Briggs because I spent time as a buffalo hunter before I took to guiding wagon trains for a living." He eyed Fargo critically. "I was up yonder, scouting for a spot to stop, when I heard a shot. Are you giving these fine folks grief? If you are, you'll have to answer to me."

Fargo bristled at the threat and started to answer, but the redhead beat him to the punch.

"This man didn't do anything except protect himself, Briggs. Tyler jumped him without provocation."

"I told the lad to be on the watch for savages, Miss Howard," the wagon boss said rather stiffly. "He was just doing his job. I can't fault him for that."

"Tyler is lucky Mr. Fargo didn't kill him," Molly said.

Briggs seemed to tense. "Who did you say?" he asked, gazing intently at Skye.

"Fargo. This gentleman's name is Skye Fargo," Molly elaborated. "Why? Do you know him?"

"I know *of* him," Briggs said, and he did not sound pleased, although his mouth curved in a smile. He shoved his right hand out. "So you're Skye Fargo, the scout and Indian fighter. I've heard that you're almost as good as Kit Carson, and I'm honored to make your acquaintance, sir.''

Puzzled by the man's behavior, Fargo shook.

"You're an Indian fighter?'' Pete asked, and nodded at the wagon boss. "Then you must have heard all about Mr. Briggs. He killed Chief Gray Wolf and twelve Sioux at the battle of Webster Pass.''

"Oh?'' Fargo said.

"Yes, sir,'' Pete said, his chin bobbing in excitement. "We heard all about it in Kansas City. It's one of the reasons we hired him to lead us to Denver.''

Buffalo Briggs cleared his throat. "I'm certain Mr. Fargo doesn't want to be bored listening to you relate my exploits, Peter.'' He shifted and clapped his hands. "Now let's get back to our wagons, folks. I wasn't able to find any cover, so we'll make camp right here and wait for the snow to stop.'' He motioned for them to move off.

"What about you, Mr. Fargo?'' Molly inquired. "Would you care to join us?''

"Yeah, please do,'' Pete added. "We'll need all the help we can get if any hostiles pay us a visit.''

The wagon boss looked at Pete sharply. "We can handle any bucks hankering to give us trouble,'' he stated. "Fargo probably has business elsewhere, and we don't want to detain him.''

Skye saw both Molly and Pete stare at him expectantly. By all rights, given the manner in which he'd been treated so far, he should mount up and ride off. He owed these people nothing, and Briggs clearly didn't want his company. But he hesitated, his mind awhirl with questions. Who was this Buffalo Briggs? In all his years on the frontier, Skye had never heard of him. Nor had he ever heard about the battle of Webster Pass. He didn't even know of a pass by that name. His intuition told him something was wrong here, and his curiosity prompted him to find out what it was.

"Please join us,'' Molly stressed, and reached out to touch his forearm. "We'd be delighted to have you ride with us for as long as you want.''

Briggs made an impatient gesture. "We don't want to impose on Mr. Fargo, my dear. He's a man of the open spaces and

17

likes his privacy, I'd wager. If he'd rather go on, it's his affair."

The man's condescending attitude rankled Fargo. In fact, practically everything about Buffalo Briggs rubbed him the wrong way. He peered up into the swirling snow, which now qualified as a first-rate blizzard, and came to a decision. "I'd be happy to join you," he said.

Molly beamed, then brushed snow from her bangs. "I have hot coffee in my wagon if you'd care to join me."

"Much obliged," Fargo said, and walked to the Ovaro. He took the stallion's reins and waited for Molly to take the lead.

"Pardon me," Pete said. "Is there any chance I could have my gun back? I just bought it in Kansas City and I don't think I've fired it ten times."

"I don't see why not," Fargo said, forking the iron over. He trailed Molly toward the wagons, passing the wagon boss, and swore he could feel the man's eyes bore into his back. It was an uncomfortable sensation, as if he'd turned his back on a rattler coiled to strike.

What had he gotten himself into? he wondered.

2

There were seven large wagons, but they weren't the typical prairie schooners used by settlers on their way west. These were enclosed affairs with high seats and small wheels, much like the vans used by patent-medicine drummers and gypsies. Shouting drivers were busily forming the vans into a large circle around a huddled group of men and women. The drivers had to yell because they couldn't see more than ten feet due to the heavy sheet of whipping snow, and there was a danger of colliding.

Molly halted well clear of the wagons and waited for them to complete the maneuver. She wrapped part of the shawl around the lower half of her face to ward off the wind. "I wish I'd grabbed my coat when I ran out. I'm pretty near froze."

"You might get frostbit," Fargo said, and draped an arm over her shoulders. She started, began to pull away, then relaxed and pressed her side flush with his. He turned so the wind struck him, not her.

"My, aren't you the gallant gentleman."

Skye couldn't tell if she was being sarcastic or not but gave her the benefit of the doubt. "I hope you folks have plenty of food, because you're going to be stuck here a spell."

"You don't think the storm will end soon?"

"This is a blue norther, ma'am. We'll be lucky if the snow stops in three days."

"But Buffalo assured us it would pass quickly," Molly said anxiously.

Fargo made no reply. He didn't want to criticize the wagon boss until he learned more about the man and knew how she felt about him. One thing was obvious, though. Any wagon boss worthy of the title would know that the blizzard would last indefinitely and that these people were in a real tight fix. Either Briggs knew and didn't want to alarm them, or else Briggs had no business hiring out to guide folks across the plains to the Rockies. Most wagon bosses were skilled plainsmen who knew all the trails by heart, knew all the places to find water, all the rivers and streams and springs, and knew how to avoid all the regions where hostile Indians were likely to make trouble. Fargo had heard of a few greenhorns who had tried to pass themselves off as competent wagon bosses; they seldom lasted more than a few months and invariably many trusting souls perished with them.

The wooden vans formed the circle swiftly. As one clattered past, Fargo thought he detected writing on the side but couldn't be certain. When the wagons finally stopped and the men clambered down, he moved forward between two of them, the stallion on his heels.

The men went to work unhitching the teams and leading the animals into the middle of the circle, while the other people entered various wagons.

"Follow me," Molly said, hastening to a van on the right. She opened the door at the back and climbed in.

Fargo stepped around the corner to a rear wheel and tied the Ovaro. Giving the pinto a pat, he said, "I'll be back in a bit," and went into the wagon. The interior was roomier than he would have imagined and deliciously warm thanks to a potbellied stove at the front. A considerable pile of wood had been stacked to the right of the stove. Two narrow bunks on either side afforded sleeping and seating accommodations. Lining the walls, piled on top of one another, were suitcases and chests for clothes and such.

Molly walked directly to the stove and extended her hands to within inches of the hot metal. "Oh, this is wonderful. Come warm yourself, Mr. Fargo."

"Call me Skye," he told her, nodding to the two other occupants of the van, a portly man in a fancy suit and an older woman in a fine calico dress. They were seated across from each other, and they regarded him with friendly expressions.

"My word, where did this gentleman come from, Molly?" the woman asked in a distinctly southern accent.

Molly launched into a brief explanation, concluding with

"Skye, I'd like to introduce Chelsea Mosby and Kevin O'Casey, two of the more seasoned members of our troupe."

O'Casey walked up to Fargo and offered his hand. "Pleased to be meetin' you," he said in a thick Irish brogue, then promptly switched to perfect English. "You must be as daft as this troupe to be abroad in this rotten weather."

"You folks couldn't have picked a worse time to travel," Fargo agreed, shaking, and asked, "What is this about a troupe?"

"We're actors," O'Casey said. "Part of the Frederick Repertory Troupe out of Chicago. Been hitting the boards now nigh on seven months, and frankly I pine for the Windy City. It's not Dublin, but it sure as hell beats the middle of the plains in the middle of winter."

A feather could have floored Fargo. A company of actors! No wonder they didn't know what they were doing. And no wonder they were blindly following Briggs. They had no idea if he was guiding them wisely or not.

"Don't look so shocked, Mr. Fargo," Chelsea said. "It's not unheard of for acting companies to travel to the frontier towns and cities."

"I know, ma'am," Fargo said. Entertainment was at a premium west of the Mississippi River. Since the settlers, miners, soldiers, and others inhabiting the West were often starved for diversions, hefty profits were reaped by those companies hardy enough to venture to the remote areas to put on shows. Denver, with its hordes of miners and constant influx of pilgrims, had become a prime stopping point for many of the traveling shows.

"We're slated to perform in Dever for two weeks," O'Casey said. "Then it's back to Chicago, back to the grand comforts of civilization, to fine whiskey and fine food and hot baths." He sighed. "I, for one, can hardly wait."

"Your problem, Kevin," Chelsea said, "is that you've grown too soft. If you can't spent an hour in a tub every day, you think your life is ruined."

O'Casey pressed a hand to his chest and grimaced as if in great pain. "You cut me to the quick, darlin'. And to think you suckled me at your bosom."

Light laughter burst from Molly. "Pay no attention to him, Skye. Chelsea played his mother once in a play we put on, and he's never let her forget it." She indicated a small table to the left of the stove on which rested a coffeepot and several cups. "Care for that coffee now?"

"In a bit," Fargo said. "I've got to tend to my horse first."

"A true Westerner," O'Casey said with a smile.

"Later I'll take you over to meet Tom Frederick," Molly offered. "He's been laid up for two days with stomach problems. The poor man can't keep a bite of food down."

Fargo exited the van, closing the door behind him. He walked around the wagon, then halted in bewilderment at finding the Ovaro gone. Gazing right and left revealed only a wall of snow. The wind howled mercilessly. He thought he'd tied the reins tight enough to prevent the stallion from pulling loose, but apparently he hadn't. He walked toward the middle of the circle and found where the other horses were tethered. They were huddled closely together for warmth, their backsides to the screaming wind. Making a circuit of the animals, he failed to see the stallion.

Where could the Ovaro have gone?

None of the troupe members was outside, and he didn't blame them. The temperature had continued to plummet. A person could freeze in minutes if not careful. He wasn't about to ask their help anyway, because the pinto was his problem. Returning to Molly's wagon, he searched for tracks, not expecting to find any. Fate smiled on him. Perhaps due to the van blocking off some of the wind, there were a number of readable prints near the wheel. And there, plain as the nose on his face, were boot prints left by someone who had walked up to the wheel and apparently untied the stallion.

Skye was furious. Who would do such a harebrained thing? Maybe, he speculated, someone had intended to bed the Ovaro with the other horses but the stallion ran off and the person gave chase. He followed the tracks to the end of the wagon, where the blowing snow had already erased them. Squaring his shoulders and tugging his hat low over his brow, he walked into the open. In such weather the Ovaro wouldn't have gone far. He should find it nearby.

Sticking two fingers in his mouth, Fargo vented a loud whistle. The wind smothered the sound before it could carry more than a few feet. He walked out farther, the snow battering his face like stinging sand. Suddenly he heard a slight sound to his rear and went to turn, but a strong arm abruptly looped around his neck and clamped on his windpipe. Someone yanked him backward, off balance, and he wrenched to the right in an effort to dislodge his attacker. The motion saved his life.

A knife lanced into Skye's side, its aim thrown off by his movement, tearing through his buckskins and ripping open his skin but not sinking deep. The blade missed vital organs.

Fargo swung his left elbow around and in and connected with his attacker's ribs. There was a low grunt and the grip on his throat slackened a bit. He swung again swiftly, brutally, not giving his attacker a breather, knowing he was lost if he hesitated. Again the man behind him grunted, and then Fargo got both feet firmly on the ground and shoved backward. The combination of his weight, the momentum of his shove, and the slippery snow underfoot caused the man to stumble rearward, carrying Fargo back with him. The arm around Skye's neck let go and the man moved out from behind him.

Gravity took over. Fargo went down, agony searing his side, and landed on his back. Instantly he scrambled upright and clawed at the Colt, spinning to confront his adversary. Only there was no one to confront. He glimpsed a blurred form vanishing in the snow and took two impetuous strides in pursuit. Acute pain drew him up short. He slipped his hand under his sheepskin coat and shirt and contacted sticky blood. His blood. Lots of it, too.

Already the man had disappeared. Fargo didn't bother to go after him. It wouldn't do to blunder into the bastard's gun sights, and the pain would dull his reflexes. Reluctantly, he stepped toward Molly's wagon, then halted when he heard a thud to his rear. Thinking there might be two assailants, he whirled, his thumb cocking the .44.

The Ovaro, covered with downy white, walked up to him and nuzzled his cheek.

"So here you are," Fargo said softly. "That varmint must have tried to run you off, but you wouldn't go." He stroked the stallion's neck. "Good boy." Taking the reins in his left hand, he led the horse to the middle of the circle where the other animals were gathered. Despite the discomfort, he removed the saddle and bedroll, then tethered the Ovaro with the rest. The horses would be all right for the time being. Huddled together as they were, their bodies would keep them warm. Later he would find food for the stallion.

Carrying saddle and bedroll, Fargo returned to the wagon and rapped on the door. His back and buttocks felt slick and clammy. When the door opened, he went to enter and suffered a bout of weakness.

Kevin O'Casey stood to one side of the door. "Is something the matter, man?" he inquired when the big man slumped. "Here, let me give you a hand." Bending down, he grabbed the saddle and pulled it inside.

"Thanks," Fargo said, and took a deep breath. He entered and deposited his bedroll against the wall. Only then did he shuck the sheepskin coat.

O'Casey, in the act of closing the door, looked over and whistled in alarm. "Begorra, boyo! What the hell happened to ye?" he asked, reverting to his Irish brogue in the exigency of the moment.

"Skye?" Molly asked, coming over, her features lined in concern.

"Some polecat jumped me," Fargo explained, and yanked the bottom edge of his shirt out from under his gunbelt, then lifted the shirt and craned his head so he could see the wound clearly. Two inches of torn flesh were exposed, his blood seeping over the bottom of the neat incision.

"My Lord!" Chelsea exclaimed, horrified.

"Was it an Indian?" O'Casey asked.

"No," Fargo said.

"Are you saying someone from our troupe did this?" Chelsea inquired skeptically. "That's impossible."

"An Indian would have gone straight for my throat or my heart," Fargo explained. "And he wouldn't have given up until one of us was dead." He frowned at the wound. "No, a white man did this, and the only men hereabouts are those in this outfit."

24

Molly spun on her heels and hurried to the table near the stove. "Who did it isn't important right now. The important thing is to clean that nasty cut and stop the flow of blood." She glanced at Chelsea. "Don't we have some medical supplies in one of our chests?"

Chelsea nodded. "I believe we do. I'll find them," she said, stepping to a chest along the right-hand wall.

"Why don't you have a seat?" O'Casey suggested.

Fargo didn't need any prompting. He'd lost a lot of blood and felt uncommonly weak. Taking a seat on the nearest bunk, he removed his hat and stripped off his shirt.

"Why would anyone want to stab you?" O'Casey wondered.

"When I know the answer to that, I'll know who to kill," Fargo said.

Molly, in the act of bringing over a tin of hot water and a clean towel, cast a disapproving gaze at him. "Kill? You actually intend to hunt the man down and shoot him?"

"Shoot him. Knife him. Whatever it takes," Fargo said, wincing as a spasm jolted his torso.

"How very barbaric," Molly commented, kneeling beside him. She began cleaning the cut, pressing gingerly with the wet towel, her face scrunched up. "An eye for an eye, is that it?"

"Am I supposed to sit around and wait for this son of a bitch to finish the job?" Skye snapped.

"No. Report the incident to the authorities in Denver," Molly proposed. "They're the ones who should handle it."

"Where are you from?" Fargo asked.

"I was born and raised in Philadelphia. Why?"

"Figured as much. Is this your first trip into this country?"

Molly nodded while carefully wiping blood from a corner of the wound.

"Then you have a lot to learn about the way of life out here," Fargo said. "In the first place, there isn't all that much law west of Kansas. There are town marshals and a few county sheriffs in the more civilized areas, but for the most part there are thousands of square miles where there is no law enforcement whatsoever. And federal marshals are as scarce as hen's teeth."

"And in the second place?" Molly asked, locking her eyes on his.

"Out here a man learns to saddle his own horse. If it's a bronc, he'd better know how to ride it or he'll wind up with busted bones."

"Meaning, I suppose, that every man is responsible for his own actions and must bear the consequences of those actions?"

"And every woman."

After studying him for a few seconds, Molly said softly, "You're a hard man, Skye Fargo."

"It's a hard land."

Chelsea walked over bearing a brown leather valise. "The medical stuff is in here," she announced, "but don't ask me what all there is. Adams packed a valise for each wagon and I didn't see him do it."

"Let's take a look," Molly said, gripping the handle and lowering the valise to the floor. Opening it, she reached in and pulled out a roll of white linen bandage. "This is just what we need."

Fargo closed his eyes and pondered while she ministered to the cut. The attempt on his life made no sense. So far as he knew, he didn't have any enemies in the acting company. But then he hadn't met all of them yet, and perhaps there was one who knew him from somewhere or was related to someone he'd gunned down in a long-forgotten gunfight.

Outside, the wind howled with increasing volume. The blizzard raged in all its elemental fury. He wasn't going anywhere for a spell, which meant the killer would have plenty of opportunities to remedy his earlier failure. Unless he wanted to wind up as prairie-grass fertilizer, he must stay alert every waking moment and sleep like a mountain lion being tracked by bloodhounds—light and ready to fight at the least little noise.

"I should report this affair to Briggs and Mr. Frederick," O'Casey said, grabbing a heavy coat off a hook on one wall. "They'll want to know." He moved to the door, waved, and slid out into the blistering cold. A strong gust blew in before he got the door closed again.

"Brrrr!" Chelsea said. "I've never known weather so cold, not even in Chicago." She crossed her arms and vigorously rubbed her shoulders. "How do living things survive the winters out here?"

"The critters and Indians make do," Fargo said without opening his eyes. Whether from fatigue or the loss of blood, he felt an odd lethargy and resisted an urge to curl up into a ball and fall asleep.

"At least we don't have to worry about the Indians bothering us now," Chelsea remarked. "They must stay in their tepees during such wicked storms."

"Not always," Fargo told her. "Indians aren't as bothered by cold and heat as most whites. They live outdoors all of their lives, and they learn early how to live in conditions you couldn't abide." He idly scratched his chin. "Once, years ago, I saw some Sioux children playing on a frozen river. It was close to zero, but many of them hardly had any clothes on. Some were naked. Yet the cold didn't affect them at all."

"I'm glad I wasn't born a Sioux," Chelsea said. "They sound downright primitive."

Fargo could have informed her that the Sioux were his friends and some of the most noble people on the face of the planet. He could have told her that Sioux parents were loving and kind, that Sioux children were reared to be upstanding members of the tribe. He could have said that the Sioux, in many respects, were less primitive than the whites who so stridently condemned all Indians, that the Sioux weren't as beset by greed and lust and envy as the whites, but he didn't. Why waste his breath to convince her of facts she would have to experience for herself in order to believe?

Molly worked on, dressing the wound and wrapping the long linen bandage around his body several times, covering the slash, before tying it securely on the side opposite. She had just finished and stood up when the door was thrown wide and in stalked the wagon boss trailed by Kevin O'Casey.

The blast of frigid air revived Fargo, who had been close to dozing. He sat erect, his right hand dropping to his thigh within inches of his gun butt, and he faced the wagon boss squarely.

"What's this about you being attacked, Fargo?" Buffalo Briggs asked brusquely, staring straight at the bandage.

"Some owl-hoot jumped me," Fargo said with as much contempt as he could muster.

Brigg's mouth twitched, his lips compressing into a thin line.

Then he hitched at his gunbelt and said, "Any idea who it was?"

"Not at the moment. But I'll find the bastard before too long."

"I don't want you bothering the folks in this wagon train," Briggs said defensively. "If you go around asking a lot of questions, it will upset some of them."

"Tough," Fargo said, and slowly rose. The wagon boss took a step backward. "I aim to stick with this train until Denver, and by then I'll likely have my man."

Briggs clearly resented Skye's attitude. His dark eyes betrayed intense hatred, inexplicable in light of the fact that Skye hardly knew him. "I decide who rides with us and who doesn't," he said, "and I don't care much for your company."

The gauntlet had been flung at Fargo's feet. He didn't like any man to prod him, least of all a dandy with an ego the size of Pike's Peak. And he wasn't about to leave the train for any reason. "I'm staying," he announced calmly, "and there isn't a damn thing you can do about it."

Buffalo Briggs glowered and puffed out his chest. Suddenly, without warning, he made a play for his six-guns.

3

It was no contest.

Fargo had the big Colt out and leveled at the man's midsection in the time it took the wagon boss to grip those shiny ivory handles and begin to pull. Briggs became as rigid as a tree, his eyes wide in astonishment, his mouth forming an oval the size of an apple. His thumb on the hammer, Fargo said coolly, "Make your play and they'll need a new wagon boss come morning."

All the starch and bluster in Briggs evaporated. He blinked, then ever so slowly removed his hands from his hardware and eased them in front of his body, palms out. "No one ever told me you were such a gun hand."

"Use something often enough and you get good at it," Fargo said. His voice hardened. "If you ever try to draw on me again, I won't be so charitable." With a quick flip of his hand he twirled the Colt into its holster.

"You've made your point," Briggs said. "I'm not about to buck you again." He started to turn away.

"Not so fast."

Pausing, apprehension mirrored in his beady eyes, Briggs licked his lips. "What do you want?"

"Where's your knife?"

"My what?"

"Don't stall. Every man owns a knife. Where's yours?" Fargo probed. Of all the people on the wagon train, the wagon boss was his prime suspect. If he examined the knife and found blood, he'd have the would-be assassin.

Briggs seemed genuinely surprised by the question. "Sure, I've got me an old Bowie, but I hardly ever use it. The blamed thing is too heavy to carry everywhere. I think it's in my saddlebags over in my wagon."

Fargo hadn't seen the knife the attacker wielded, but it

29

definitely hadn't been a Bowie. Named after the famous knife fighter who died heroically at the Alamo, Bowies were huge knives capable of gutting a man in a single swipe. If his attacker had used one, Fargo would have been ripped open from his waist to his ribs. "That's the only knife you own?"

"Yes," Briggs said. "What are you—?" he started to ask, and caught himself when the obvious answer occurred to him. His face flushed. "I wasn't the one who stabbed you, Fargo. I'm not the type to jump a man from behind."

How did the wagon boss know he'd been attacked from the rear? Fargo wondered. Briggs hadn't seen the wound, so he had no way of judging the angle of penetration. Skye's suspicions heightened, but he made no comment. Suspicions weren't proof, and he'd need concrete evidence before he could accuse the man outright.

Briggs looked at the women, touched his hat brim, and departed, slamming the door in his wake.

"You have an enemy there, boyo," Kevin O'Casey remarked. "Were I you, I'd be going around with one eye over my shoulder at all times."

"Where did you people run into him?" Fargo asked.

Molly answered. "In Chicago. Mr. Frederick introduced Briggs to us when he announced we'd be going on tour to Kansas City and points west."

"Do you know where Frederick met him?"

"No. Why? Is it important?"

"Could be," Fargo said, and let the matter drop for the time being. But he intended to find out everything he could about this so-called wagon master who didn't have the good sense to wear his pistols underneath his coat in a snowstorm. "How many of you folks are there?"

"Twenty-two, not counting the teamsters," Molly said. "We're one of the largest touring companies there is," she added proudly.

Fargo was more interested in the other bit of information. "How many teamsters do you have?"

"Two. They both hired on with Buffalo Briggs and work for him," Molly replied. "They chop wood and tote water and take turns driving one of the wagons."

"I don't like either of them," Chelsea declared.

Skye turned toward her. "Why not?"

"They're mean men. You can see it in their eyes. And one of them, Grimes his name is, can't keep his eyes off us ladies. Why, he even ogled me."

O'Casey laughed. "You wish he did, darling. I think your imagination is getting the better of you. He's always been polite and proper around me."

"You're a man, Kevin. You wouldn't understand."

"Do these teamsters pack hardware?" Fargo inquired.

"Guns?" Chelsea said. "Why, yes, they do. They both wear revolvers, and Grimes has a big knife he uses for whittling and such."

Interesting, Fargo reflected. He'd have to question this Grimes at the earliest opportunity. "Why is your wagon train so far from the Solomon Trail?"

"What trail?" Molly said.

"The Solomon River Trail. It'll take you almost clear across Kansas Territory," Fargo explained. "It's not as well traveled as the Oregon Trail, the Platte River Trail, or the Santa Fe Trail, but I figure it's the one you're taking to Denver, since it's the closest."

"I don't know much about trails," Molly said. "We've relied totally on Mr. Briggs's discretion, and he told us shortly before you showed up that we are right where we should be."

"If you're heading for Mexico," Fargo said. The more he learned about Buffalo Briggs, the more convinced he became the man was a phoney. What did Briggs hope to gain by passing himself off as a competent wagon boss? The pay couldn't be high enough to justify the deception.

Kevin O'Casey coughed nervously. "Uh, boyo, I hope you won't mind my bringing this up, but where are you going to sleep tonight? This particular wagon is reserved for Molly, Chelsea, and Abigail. I was just visiting Chelsea when you popped in."

Molly grinned at Fargo and winked. "We have an extra bunk, Kevin, and I, for one, wouldn't mind the extra company."

"You can't be serious, lass," O'Casey said, sounding

shocked at the notion. "Think of the talk. Having a man stay over is something Abby might do, but not you."

"Abby goes after anything in pants," Chelsea said, sitting on the edge of a bunk. "So you'd better watch yourself, Mr. Fargo. She's over at one of the wagons visiting her current beau, Dan Huglin, but she should be back soon."

The Irishman moved closer to the Trailsman. "You're welcome to stay in the same wagon I do. All the bunks are filled, but there are plenty of blankets and you could spread out near the stove."

"Would the other men object?" Fargo asked.

"Not at all. One of them is Tom Frederick, by the way."

"Then I'll do it," Fargo stated, eager to question the leader of the troupe about Buffalo Briggs. He donned his coat, grabbed his bedroll, and moved toward his saddle, but O'Casey picked it up before he could.

"You shouldn't be carrying this in your condition," Kevin said.

"I'm grateful," Fargo said, stepping nearer so he could scoop the Sharps from the scabbard. "Now I'm set." He gazed at Molly. "I'll look you up in the morning."

"Do that. I'll still be here," she said, smiling.

Fargo was a pace behind O'Casey as the Irishman made for the door, when with another stiff gust of icy air the door opened and in bounded a blonde sprite bundled in a heavy wool coat.

"God! I will never, ever leave Chicago again! This miserable excuse for a tour is the worst I've ever been on. My *derrière* practically froze just walking between wagons!" she stated in a rush of words, then caught herself and stared in mild surprise at Fargo. "Hello? What's this? You must be the one everybody is talking about."

"Hello, Abby," O'Casey said.

The blonde ignored him. She opened her coat, exposing a shapely body in a clinging green dress, and sashayed up to Skye. "I'm Abby Spabel, and I'm delighted to meet you." She held out her hand.

Fargo had to tuck the Sharps under his right arm in order to shake. "Skye Fargo, ma'am."

32

She gave his fingers a firm squeeze, then traced a fingertip across his palm.

"I've heard about you. Sorry I missed all the commotion, but I was with a . . . friend," Abby said, her rosy lips curling coquettishly. "I do so hope you'll be with us awhile."

"I plan to be."

Abby admired the spread of his broad shoulders and his slim hips. "I will say one thing for the West. The men out here are enough to give a woman naughty dreams."

"Abby," Chelsea said, "why don't you pretend to have morals and behave yourself. You hardly know the man."

"I'm sure I'll remedy that oversight," Abby declared, lowering her hand and sliding to one side. "I take it you gentlemen are leaving?"

"Correct, my dear," Kevin said, exiting.

Fargo was about to do likewise when Abby placed a restraining hand on his arm. "Don't be a stranger, big man. This trip is enough to bore a rock, and I could use a little excitement."

"I'll keep it in mind, ma'am," Fargo said, and out of the corner of his eye he observed Molly's features briefly harden. He went out quickly, shutting the door as he did. A burst of wind about took his hat off and chilled him to the marrow. The temperature, he guessed, was now well below zero and would bottom out at twenty below by morning.

O'Casey stood waiting, stamping his feet in the six-inch-deep snow and puffing tiny clouds. "Hurry, man. I can't abide his cold."

They went across the enclosed area, passing the horses along the way. Fargo was pleased to see the Ovaro huddled with the other horses and reminded himself to feed the stallion soon.

"Some of the wagons have four occupants, some have only three," O'Casey was saying. "Frederick assigned each of us a bunk and we're stuck with it. I think he tried to bunk together those who would best get along."

"How many of the troupe are women?" Fargo asked.

"Seven. There are four in another wagon besides the three you've met."

"What about Briggs? Where does he sleep?"

"In a wagon with the two teamsters and young Tyler. Why?"

"Nothing," Fargo said, although he found it curious that Briggs had selected the greenhorn Tyler to serve as guard when there were older men in the troupe who might have been a shade less trigger-happy. They came to a wagon and the Irishman entered without knocking. Skye stepped into the warm interior and automatically closed the door to prevent much of the warmth from escaping.

There were two men present. Seated on a bunk on the right was Pete, busily reading a magazine. He glanced up, did a double take, and stood. Lying in a bunk on the left was a skinny man whose pale skin accented his black handlebar mustache and dark eyes. A blanket was pulled up to his chin.

"Gentlemen," O'Casey said, "this here is Skye Fargo, and he'll be staying with us awhile."

"We've already met," Pete said.

The man on his back lifted his head and managed a wan smile of greeting. "Hello. I'm Tom Frederick, the head of this company. Excuse me for not standing, but I've been as weak as a kitten for a couple of days now. Stomach problems."

"I understand," Fargo replied, placing his gear in a corner. O'Casey put the saddle next to his bedroll.

"Pete told me what happened with Tyler," Frederick said. "I'm truly sorry. I can't imagine what came over the youngster. He wouldn't harm a flea before we left Chicago."

"He's been hanging around Briggs and those teamsters too much," Kevin said, walking to the stove.

"Don't speak badly of Buffalo. He's doing the best he can under the circumstances," Frederick stated.

"I wouldn't be so sure," Kevin replied testily.

"Why are you being so critical of him?" the troupe leader wanted to know.

O'Casey gave him an account of the knife attack on Fargo and the confrontation between Skye and the wagon boss.

"My word," Frederick said when the Irishman was done. He struggled to rise on his elbows and stared at the big man. "I'm at a loss to explain any of this, but I can assure you no one in my company was responsible for the attempt on your life."

34

"Know them all that well, do you?" Fargo asked.

"Fairly well, yes. Most have worked for me for a year or more."

"I know why all this is happening," Pete unexpectedly asserted, and rose. "It's the damn jinx. That's what it is."

"Don't start with that nonsense again," O'Casey said.

Tom Frederick noted their guest's quizzical gaze. "Some of the troupe have concocted a wild theory that we're under a jinx, Mr. Fargo," he explained. "Actors and actresses are by their very nature a highly superstitious lot, and all it takes is one or two small accidents to make them grab for their lucky rabbit's foot."

"I wouldn't label two deaths as small accidents," Pete said resentfully.

"What deaths?" Fargo inquired, all attention.

"Before we left Chicago one of our company died," Pete answered. "Jack Wehner, the man in charge of our props, fell from on high while setting up the overhead lights. The police believed he simply slipped. I knew Jack well. He was like a monkey up there. If he slipped, I'm the Queen of Sheba."

"Who else died?"

O'Casey answered. "That would be Bill Schweer, a fine actor from Connecticut. We were four days out of Kansas City when he was slain by redskins."

"You saw him be killed?"

"No, actually none of us did," Kevin said. "It happened at night after we'd made camp. He liked to stroll about for a nip of fresh air before retiring. Well, he hadn't been gone five minutes when we heard this terrible scream. We found him with a freshly made spear sticking out of his chest. Poor devil."

Fargo removed his coat while pondering the new disclosures. He doubted Schweer had been slain by Indians. There were no hostile tribes dwelling within a four-day ride of Kansas City. The Cheyennes hunted in the western part of the Territory, but their war parties shied away from eastern Kansas because the army patrols from Fort Leavenworth were particularly numerous in that region. As well the patrols should be, since there were many more settlers in the eastern section than in the west. "You say it was a freshly made spear?"

Tom Frederick nodded. "It was no more than a long tree limb sharpened at one end. Buffalo Briggs told us the Kansas Indians sometimes use such weapons."

The Kansas tribe? The ones the Territory was named after? They had never given the whites a lick of trouble. Fargo hung his coat on a hook. "Did you send a rider back to Kansas City to report the death?"

"No," Frederick said. "Buffalo said it would be too dangerous with the whole Kansas tribe on the war path. We buried Schweer on a knoll and read from the Good Book."

Fargo thoughtfully crossed to the stove to warm his hands. There could be no doubt that Buffalo Briggs was a fake, but how could he convince the acting company of that fact? It would be Briggs's word against his, and Frederick had a high opinion of the fraud.

"Has anyone fed the horses yet?" Frederick inquired.

"I saw the teamsters feeding them awhile ago," Pete said.

The reminder jarred Fargo. He chided himself for being so forgetful and hurried to slip into his coat. "My horse needs feed. Do you have any feed you can spare?"

"We have oats stockpiled in Briggs's wagon," Frederick said. "You're welcome to help yourself to some."

"Obliged," Fargo said. "Which wagon is it?"

"I'll show you, boyo," O'Casey volunteered.

"Just tell me which one it is," Fargo said. "You don't have to go out in the blizzard again."

"I don't mind," Kevin said, going out first and drawing his coat tight around him. He didn't speak again until the door was closed. "I saw the look on your face when Schweer was mentioned. In your opinion, were Indians responsible?"

"No."

"I've had my doubts. So have a few of the others. But none of us said anything because Briggs is the expert. We all assumed he should know."

"Briggs doesn't know his asshole from a prairie-dog burrow," Fargo said. "Show me where his wagon is parked. I have a few questions I want to ask him."

The Irishman walked rapidly toward another van. "You be careful, Skye. Grimes and the other teamster, Vangent, will probably be with Briggs. And you heard what Chelsea said about Grimes. If she's right, he's a dangerous man.''

Fargo made no comment, but his right hand strayed to his Colt and loosened it in his holster.

4

The door handle chilled Fargo's left palm as he twisted and shoved the door wide. Inside, seated around a table and playing poker, were four men: Buffalo Briggs, the young Tyler, a hatchet-faced hombre with a knife on his left hip who must be Grimes, and a stocky man in a greasy shirt who had to be Vangent. Buffalo Briggs was facing the doorway, in the act of dealing, and his hands froze as he laid eyes on Skye.

"You!" Briggs blurted.

Fargo strode almost to the table, taking in the bunks and the stove and the supplies stacked from the floor to the ceiling. To the left were two bins of feed with bags hanging next to them. The other men turned to appraise him, young Tyler the only one who smiled in greeting. There was blatant hostility in Grimes's eyes and wariness in Vangent's.

"What do you want?" the wagon boss demanded.

"Tom Frederick said I could help myself to some oats," Fargo said.

"This feed is for our animals, not for the convenience of strays that happen by," Briggs said.

The insult was clear. Fargo walked over and removed an empty feed bag from the wall, then faced the table. "If any of you gents care to try and stop me, go right ahead."

Briggs slapped his cards down on the table top but made no move to rise. Nor did the teamsters, although the one called Grimes, judging by his baleful expression, was sorely tempted to dispute the issue. His hard eyes glittered with spite and his thin lips twitched with suppressed violent urges.

O'Casey, who had stayed near the entrance, spoke in Skye's defense. "I was present when Mr. Frederick gave his permission," he announced. "And since Mr. Frederick was the one who insisted on bringing the feed and paid for it with troupe funds, you have no grounds, Briggs, for refusing Mr. Fargo.''

"As if I care," Buffalo Briggs said angrily, his tone belying his statement.

Fargo began scooping oats into the feed bag. "I heard about Bill Schweer," he mentioned casually, and glancing at Briggs saw the wagon boss visibly tense. "I also heard you blamed his death on the Kansas Indians."

"What about it?" Briggs snapped.

"Oh, nothing. Except that the Kansas Indians are just about the most peaceable tribe on the plains. There hasn't been one report of them ever attacking a white man. Strange that they would start on the war path now when they practically live in the shadow of Fort Leavenworth."

Briggs shifted and glared. "I never claimed the whole damn tribe was on the war path. It could have been a few bucks out to count coup."

"That's odd. Frederick told me that you did say the tribe was on the war trail."

"He must have misunderstood."

Fargo took his sweet time filling the feed bag. He enjoyed making the wagon boss sweat, and from the nervous manner in which Briggs kept stroking his chin and picking at the fringe on his buckskins, he was succeeding. Perhaps he could force Briggs into revealing his hand by applying the right amount of pressure. "Strange the Kansas bucks would take to counting coup now when they've been farmers for more years than I can recollect."

"Are you calling me a liar?" Briggs growled, placing a hand on the top of the chair as if about to stand.

Pivoting, Fargo smiled and said in a deceptively normal voice, "I reckon I am."

Tension charged the van. Briggs, Grimes, and Vangent were coiled to surge erect. Young Tyler appeared bewildered by the turns of events and Kevin gaped.

"I don't know what your game is," Fargo told the wagon boss, "but I know you're up to no good. And as soon as I can prove it, I'll talk Frederick into firing you." He stopped and waited for them to make their play.

Briggs glowered, his hand gripping the chair so tightly that his knuckles were white. Inexplicably, he abruptly turned back to the table and resumed dealing cards. "How many did you want, Grimes?" he asked.

The card game continued as if Fargo weren't in the wagon. Skye finished filling the feed bag, dropped the scoop in the bin, and strolled to the door. He went out without a backward glance, the Irishman close behind him.

"Begorra, boyo, but you take chances. I thought for sure those three were going to pull their guns."

"They're smarter than I gave them credit for being," Fargo said, heading for the stock. "They'll bide their time and try their hand when I least expect it." The wind stabbed into him like the point of an icicle and he drew his coat close about him.

"I never met a man who likes to live as dangerously as you do," Kevin remarked.

"Would you rather I ride off and let Briggs keep doing whatever he's up to?"

"Not at all. I think your coming was a godsend meant to spare us from more needless grief."

The Ovaro didn't spy Fargo until he was a few feet off. Then the sturdy stallion moved forward, saw the feed bag, and bobbed its head in anticipation.

"Here you go," Fargo said, attaching the bag properly and listening to the pinto's big teeth crunch as it ate. He would have to return in half an hour to remove the bag. Afterward, he intended to stretch out and sleep until dawn. If, by some miracle, the snow had stopped by then, he would have a lot to do. If not, he would be stuck right where he was until Nature's fury abated.

"May I ask you a question?" Kevin inquired.

"Go ahead."

"It's sort of personal and I don't want to offend you."

Fargo looked at him. "I won't chew your head off."

"Very well," Kevin said, and took a breath. "Have you ever killed anyone?"

"Yes."

"How many would you say you've killed?"

"I have no idea. I've never counted them."

"That many?"

"That many. Why?"

"Oh, nothing," the Irishman said, tucking his collar around his neck. "But I wouldn't want to be in Buffalo Briggs's boots for all the tea in China."

Morning brought no change in the weather. A deluge of glittering flakes poured down from a completely overcast sky, adding more snow to the foot already covering the frozen ground. The wind howled nonstop, at times resembling a pack of wolves during a full moon.

Fargo started the day by feeding the Ovaro and walking it around the circle a few times, the only exercise he could give it until the storm stopped. The rest of the time he spent in the wagon.

The acting company wasn't in bad shape yet. They had an ample store of food, grain for the animals, and wood for the stoves in the large vans. Water was easy to obtain simply by melting snow.

Throughout the morning the actors and actresses braved the cold to dash from van to van, visiting with one another for a while before moving on to the next wagon. In their ignorance they were not very concerned about the blizzard. To them, it would soon blow over and they would be on their way.

Skye knew better but saw no reason to alarm them for the moment. He was pleased when the door opened and in came Molly, Chelsea, and Abby. Both Molly and Abby gave him a hug in greeting, then settled in for a spell. They talked about the theater, and how each had climbed from the lowly ranks of bit players to established performers who were recognized by the critics and appreciated by their fans. Abby, especially, went on and on about herself.

Fargo listened with half an ear, resigned to his temporary fate. So it was that he wasn't paying much attention when Abby said something he missed, and he quickly focused on her when she asked a question.

"Would you care to see them?"

"What?" he asked.

"The clippings I was telling you about, silly," Abby replied.

"I keep a scrapbook of all the reviews and the compliments I've received from my adoring public. It's in my bag in our wagon."

"Sure, I'd like to see it sometime," Fargo said, thinking it would be just about as exciting as watching a pair of frogs mate.

Abby popped to her feet and grinned. "Then how about right now?"

"This minute?"

"No, next year," Abby joked, and took his hand, pulling him off the bunk on which he sat. "You can escort me there and we'll spend a few minutes going through the scrapbook." She gazed at Molly and Chelsea. "You ladies don't mind if we leave you for a while, do you?"

"Not at all," Molly said with the same degree of warmth as the air outside.

"Don't be long," Chelsea chided. "We do so adore Mr. Fargo's pleasant company."

Fargo noticed Frederick and Kevin staring enviously at him as he shrugged into his coat and was hauled from the van by Abby. For such a little woman, she was full of vim and vinegar. She hastened to her wagon as if her britches were on fire. "What's your rush?" he asked.

"That Molly won't give us more than half an hour before she'll bring her nosy self over."

"So? A half hour is plenty of time for looking at your scrapbook."

Abby halted so abruptly he almost ran into her. She glanced up and chuckled. "You can't be as dumb as you're letting on." With a yank of his arm she kept going. "I couldn't sleep last night because of you. Tossed and turned, thinking of those broad shoulders and that handsome face."

"You don't beat around the bush, do you?"

"Life's too short to be wasting time," Abby said. "When I see something I want, I take it. Simple as that." She paused and swept the wagons with a resentful gesture. "And I'm so sick and tired of the men in this company. Two-thirds of them aren't worth my attention, and the rest don't have any idea how to fully satisfy a woman's cravings. I'm betting you do."

"Won't there be talk?"

"Who the hell cares? People have been talking about me behind my back since I was fourteen and my dear, loving uncle cornered me in the guest room. He never did understand why I didn't try to fight him off."

Fargo grinned. Here was a woman after his own heart, a woman who knew her physical needs and didn't put on airs to get them satisfied. He opened the door for her and stepped out of the icy wind. Amused, he watched her throw the bolt and toss her heavy coat to the floor. "What about the scrapbook?" he teased.

"Later, big man," Abby said, and tilted her head so her rosy lips were ripe to be kissed.

Skye obliged enthusiastically, locking his mouth on hers, letting the warmth of her lips warm his own. She yielded, her tiny tongue flicking out to lick his own, and he took off his coat and let it drop. When he broke the kiss, her eyes were closed and she was grinning like a cat that just ate a canary.

"Nice, big man. But I hope you can do better."

"I aim to please, ma'am," Fargo said, and rashly scooped her into his brawny arms. Immediately he regretted it. His wound flared with pain and he grimaced, then carried her to one of the narrow bunks and gently placed her on her back.

"Are you up to this, handsome?" Abby inquired, her eyes open now.

"We'll find out," Fargo said, removing his hat and gunbelt. He knelt by the low bunk and kissed her again, lingering this time, his right hand resting on her thigh until it wandered higher to cup a pert breast. Deep in her throat she groaned softly, and he tweaked her nipple through the fabric of her dress and her undergarments. His body flushed with heat. If the roof were to suddenly be torn off by the wind, he doubted if he would notice.

Her breath tasted minty and she wore an intoxicating perfume. He ran his hand over her body, from her breasts to the junction of her thighs, stoking her inner flames slowly. It had been a while since Kansas City and he wanted her as badly as a man parched with thirst wants a glass of cool water, but even though their time together was limited he intended to savor her for all she was worth.

Abby squirmed when he massaged her other breast and breathed into his ear. "You're good, big man. And getting better every minute."

Fargo stripped off her dress and started removing her lacy underthings. Her body was small but exquisitely shaped, her breasts in perfect proportion to her height, her hips swelling nicely above silken legs and dainty feet. Goose bumps erupted all over her skin when he traced his tongue between her breasts to her pubic mound and nibbled on her thighs.

"Ohhhhh, you make me wet inside."

"Really?" Fargo said. "I'd better check for myself." His hand swooped onto her cleft, his middle finger brushing her passion knob, and she arched her back and exhaled loudly. She'd spoken the truth. His palm became slick with her hot juices, and his middle finger found no resistance when he suddenly plunged it into her sheath.

"Oh, yes!" Abby exclaimed, her nails digging into his shoulders. "Like that! I love it!"

Skye pumped his finger in and out, building friction, her inner walls becoming tighter with every stroke. The heady scent of her sex tantalized him. He glued his mouth to her right nipple and sucked, feeling her fingers in his hair as she mashed his face into her bosom. Her breathing was heavy. Her hips moved of their own volition, adding to the sensations coursing through her. She was a firebrand, enjoying herself as fully as he was, a woman unashamed of her desires and anxious to satiate them fully.

He paused to unfasten his pants. They fell around his ankles, and he carefully squeezed onto the bunk between her legs. She looked down at his organ, her eyes hooded by lust, and smiled broadly.

"My, my, my. You're big all around, just like I hoped. Give it to me."

"Not yet," Fargo said, fondling her twin mounds. "When the time is ripe." He kissed her lips, her neck, her breasts, and her stomach. He licked her nipples, her sides, and her inner thighs. He brought her to an ecstatic pinnacle of inflamed passion, and not until she cooed and moaned and begged for him did he take his manhood in his left hand, position it at the opening to her tunnel, and ram it home.

Abby came up off the bunk as if jolted by a bolt of lightning, her arms and legs wrapping around him like iron bands.

Fargo commenced a rocking motion, ignoring the pang of protest from his side. His pelvis slapped against her buttocks with increasing urgency and she met every thrust with a counterthrust, enhancing their pleasure immeasurably.

"Harder!" Abby cried, bucking like a wild mare. "Harder, damn you!"

Gritting his teeth and tucking his elbow against his wound, Fargo gripped her shoulder with his free hand and rammed his pole into her with all the force he could muster. A familiar tingling sensation deep in his groin told him he wouldn't be able to hold off as long as he'd like, but he gamely exercised supreme self-control, wanting her to come before he did, to show her that he held the reins.

Arching her spine, Abby squealed, "Yes! Yes! Now!" Her bucking became wilder and her eyes flared in profound sexual bliss as she panted like a steam engine.

Fargo knew she was over the hump. He let himself go, let the explosion come, and quivered with the intensity of his sexual gratification. His side hurt terribly, but who the hell cared?

"Ohhhhhhh!" Abby howled, her nails raking his back.

A minute later they were both spent and slowly coasting to a stop. Fargo's heart pounded and his breath came in ragged gasps. His forehead drooped onto her breasts and her right nipple poked him in the eye. He blinked, shifted, and sighed.

"Ummm, nice," Abby purred, contentedly tracing a fingernail along the curve of his left ear. "I don't mind telling you that I've been laid by some of the best the West has to offer, and there isn't one of them who holds a candle to you."

Fargo figured she was lying but didn't refute her. He relished the aftermath of their union, feeling at peace with the world, a feeling that would last only until he hiked up his britches and went back out into the real world where the likes of Buffalo Briggs and Grimes waited to stab him in the back.

"We'll have to do this again sometime, big man," Abby said with a grin.

Skye couldn't resist teasing her. "I don't know. It wasn't all I'd hoped it would be. I reckon I'll have to give it some thought," he said, and almost screeched in agony when her long nails bit into his biceps.

"Next time, lover, I'll wear that redwood of yours down to a toothpick."

5

The blizzard raged all of that day and through the night, the snow continuing to fall in an unending stream of large white flakes. Not until midmorning of the next day did one of the troupe burst into Frederick's wagon and happily announce that the storm had finally ended and the clouds were breaking up.

Fargo spent most of the time in the van with the head of the company, the Irishman, and Pete. He learned more than he had ever cared to know about the acting profession, about how hard it was for the troupe to stay financially afloat, how one play might pack in the crowds and reap high profits while another would turn out to be a dud and their weeks or months of preparation and rehearsals wound up being wasted. He learned about the importance of wealthy patrons who contributed to the upkeep of the troupe, and how tours such as the one they were on brought modest but steady profits in every city and town they visited, simply because the frontier folk were so desperate for quality entertainment and willing to pay premium prices to see it.

Every now and then Fargo succeeded in turning the conversation around to a subject of much more importance: Buffalo Briggs. Frederick told him that Briggs appeared out of the blue one day at the Shubert Theater dressed in frontier attire. Briggs claimed to have heard from a friend that the troupe was planning a western tour and offered his services at a reasonable price to serve as guide and protector. Since it was common knowledge that the troupe was leaving, and an article had been written in the newspaper about the proposed trip, Frederick had not thought anything was amiss when Briggs showed up.

Frederick had wisely requested references, and Briggs had supplied a letter of referral from a Duke Francis von Metternick of Austria who had gone on an extended hunting trip in the West and had used Briggs as his guide. Metternick asserted that

Briggs was highly competent and an experienced plainsman.

"I'd like to see that letter if you don't mind," Fargo had said when told about it.

"I don't have it anymore," Frederick had responded. "Briggs wanted it back and I gave it to him. It was his only copy and he wanted to have it on hand to use as a future reference."

Fargo suspected the letter had been a phoney. Since Briggs most certainly was, the letter couldn't possibly be authentic. He knew trips through the rugged West were quite popular with the European nobility. Wealthy aristocrats paid top dollar for the privilege of hunting buffalo, meeting Indians, and pretending they were roughing it while traveling in a train of fifty wagons containing every comfort their money could buy. But he'd never heard of this Duke Francis von Metternick.

Now, as Fargo stepped from the stuffy confines of the van and gratefully breathed the crisp morning air, he spied Briggs and the teamsters among the stock, preparing the teams to move out, and he thought of the letter. Tom Frederick had gullibly accepted it at face value. Fargo wasn't so green. And he wondered why someone would go to all the trouble of writing the fake reference and arranging for Briggs to attach himself to the company. There must be a connection with the two deaths and the attempt on his own life, but he had no idea what it might be.

Suddenly his eyes narrowed. Grimes was slapping the Ovaro and cursing a blue streak in order to get the stallion to move. Almost every member of the acting company was standing around, waiting for the wagons to get on the move again, and many were staring at Grimes in severe disapproval. Fargo dashed through the three-foot-deep snow, gripped Grimes by the shoulder, and swung him fully around.

"What the—!" Grimes blurted.

And Fargo slugged him, a right uppercut that caught the teamster on the tip of the chin and lifted him off his feet to crash onto his back. The snow cushioned the landing and Grimes was instantly erect, snarling in fury and bunching his fists.

"No man lays a hand on me and walks away," Grimes said. "I'm going to pound you into the ground."

Fargo let his fists do his talking. He feinted with his left, causing Grimes to bring both hands up to protect his face, then slammed a right into the teamster's stomach that doubled the man in half. A flick of his right leg and his knee connected with Grimes's forehead and again the teamster went down, this time on his hands and knees, groggy and sputtering.

"Boyo! Behind you!"

At the warning from O'Casey, Fargo spun to find Vangent rushing at him, a picket pin upraised in the teamster's dirty hand with the pointed end ready to be plunged into Fargo's back. He darted to the left and the pin swished past his face. Shifting on one leg, he punched Vangent in the mouth, and when the second teamster stopped stock-still, dazed, he followed up with two swift blows to the head.

Vangent toppled.

"Here! Here! That will be enough!"

Fargo glanced up, surprised to see Frederick in the doorway of their wagon. The extra rest had obviously done him a world of good and he looked nearly recovered from his illness.

"What is the meaning of this? Why are you men behaving like common ruffians?"

"Grimes was hitting Fargo's horse," Kevin O'Casey explained.

"Yep," Pete added. "And for no reason that I could see."

Straightening, Fargo led the stallion to the wagon and brushed past Frederick to claim his gear.

The company head turned. "Since they are in my employ, I must apologize for their atrocious acts. Grimes is not a gentleman by any stretch of the imagination."

Fargo picked up his bedroll and the Sharps in one hand, then stooped to lift the saddle on high. "Grimes is a killer and you'd be smart not to turn your back on him."

"What in the world are you talking about?"

"Your man Schweer wasn't killed by any Kansas Indians. And if I were you, I'd fire Buffalo Briggs and find myself another wagon boss," Fargo advised, moving to the door.

"Why would you make such a recommendation?"

"Talk to Kevin. And call Briggs in here and tell him to follow my tracks back to the Solomon River Trail. You're running low on firewood, so I'll see if I can find a stand of trees you can chop down to carry you for a spell," Fargo said, and went to leave.

"Wait a minute," Frederick said, confused. "What is this about getting back on the trail? Mr. Briggs assured me we are right on it."

"You're miles south of where you should be. Keep on this way and you'll be performing in Mexico City instead of Denver."

"Do you mean to tell me that Buffalo Briggs has us lost?"

"*I* know where you are," Fargo said. "But I doubt whether he could find his butt with a map and lantern. If you want to keep following him, fine. The decision is yours. I'll head for the trail, keep my eyes peeled for the Cheyenne war party that has been roaming this area, and make camp at the best spot I can find. Try to catch up with me by dark."

Frederick swallowed. "Cheyenne war party?"

"Didn't Briggs tell you? A wagon train was attacked two weeks ago and five people were killed," Fargo said, and walked out. There. He'd done it. Put a seed of doubt and mistrust in Frederick's mind, which was all he could do under the circumstances. At least Frederick would be wary of Briggs and the word would spread among the rest of the troupe. If Briggs was up to no good, he'd have a hard time pulling off his scheme with the whole company watching his every move.

Skye started saddling the stallion. He smiled when Frederick bellowed for Briggs to get in the wagon, and smiled wider when Briggs walked by glaring at him. As he tied the bedroll behind the cantle a soft voice spoke.

"You be careful out there."

He turned. Molly had on a fur coat, her hands thrust into its pockets. "I expect to see you again by nightfall," he told her.

"I saw the fight. Are you all right?"

"Yes," Fargo said, struck by a strange look in her eyes, a hint of hurt, perhaps, that he couldn't explain.

"I've enjoyed our little talks," Molly said. "I hope we can have more later."

"I'd like that," Fargo said, and waited for her to bring up whatever was bothering her. When she merely stood there, he forked leather and looked down. "Be seeing you." Jerking on the reins, he rode out of the circled wagons and headed northward, making a beeline for the Solomon River Trail. By his reckoning he wouldn't reach it until well into the afternoon.

He was glad to be on his own again. Being couped up in the van had frayed his nerves. Give him the wide open spaces, the mountains and the plains, any day. And all that talk of actors and acting had about bored him to death. Why were actors so wrapped up in themselves and their profession? To them, nothing else seemed to matter.

The Ovaro was glad to be on the move again also. Fargo could tell by the way the big stallion strained to go faster, to work muscles long unused, but he held the horse in check. The deep snow would tire the pinto soon enough. Its powerful legs kicked out a spray of snow in all directions as the stallion trotted across the glistening white countryside.

Overhead the sky had virtually cleared except for a few stray clouds drifting lazily eastward. The sun blazed in all its glory, transforming the pristine mantle into a gleaming mirror. The brilliant light hurt Skye's eyes, forcing him to squint constantly, and he wished he'd had the foresight to smear the skin under his eyes with charcoal before leaving the wagon train. Such a simple precaution did a lot to stave off snow blindness, which every scout wisely avoided at all costs. Hours of exposure to the bright reflected sunlight could be too much for a man's eyes to bear, dimming his sight and causing them to water and itch. Usually the condition was temporary, but not being able to see for even five minutes might prove disastrous if a band of hostiles should appear.

So Skye kept his eyelids partially shut as he surveyed the vast vista of snow. All around him was flatland. Not so much as a hillock reared its rounded contours. The high buffalo grass was buried under the crushing weight of the snow, although here and there isolated clusters of tall weeds stood out like white thumbs. He saw little game—a hawk, some crows, and some sparrows. The latter nearly tempted him to turn aside and follow them. They were flying from east to west, and he knew they seldom strayed any great distance from cover. There must be trees to the west, but they might be as far as ten miles off and he didn't like the idea of the wagon train making such a wide detour. No, he'd keep on riding northward and hope he'd find other trees.

There were no tracks to be seen anywhere. No buffalo sign. No deer. Not so much as a coyote or a prairie-dog print. The wildlife would stay nestled in burrows and dens for a while yet, making hunting prospects poor. On he rode, the only living thing on the limitless Kansas plains. Time slipped by.

The temperature climbed to the low twenties. He unbuttoned his coat and loosened his bandanna, not at all bothered by the chilly air. While he couldn't tolerate the extremes an Indian could, he bore the heat and the cold far better than most other men simply by virtue of his many years spent in the wilderness. It also explained why his face and hands were bronzed like an Indian's skin.

At long last, after several hours of forging northward, Fargo spied trees in the distance. When he reached them, he found a large stand with heavy brush underneath, and he wound among the trunks until he came to the north side of the stand. Beyond lay more flat emptiness. The Solomon River Trail should be another two or three miles farther.

He took a break, dismounting and kicking snow off a wide patch of grass that the Ovaro could eat. Then he took a stick of beef jerky from his saddlebags, sat down on a log, and munched hungrily while thinking about Abby. She had come to the wagon the night before and invited him over for some tea, and she'd been flabbergasted when he'd declined. Why had he? Because Molly had been sitting beside him and he'd seen the fleeting resentment in her eyes? Because his back and shoulders hadn't yet healed from the raking her nails had done? Or simply because he hadn't been in the mood?

Idly gazing eastward, he abruptly tensed. In the remote distance were several small specks, no more than dots silhouetted against the horizon, but he knew those dots for what they were. Riders. Rising, he quickly took the stallion into the trees, tied the reins to a low limb, then searched until he found another limb he could easily break off. Returning to where he'd sat on the log, he used the limb to brush snow over his tracks. He did the same with the Ovaro's tracks. Finally he backed into the stand while brushing over his trail, and when he rejoined the pinto there was nothing to indicate they were there.

He yanked the Sharps out and fed a round into the chamber, then loosened the Colt in its holster so he could draw readily without having it snag. If those riders were Indians—and he would give ten-to-one odds they were—they might ride right past the trees without so much as slowing down. The job he'd done of covering his tracks would fool them if they didn't get too close to the tree line. If they came too close, they'd see the brush marks for what they were and put two and two together.

Moving to the right until he could see the dots clearly, he watched them grow and solidify into seven men on horseback. Seven Indians, all well armed. Seven Cheyenne warriors.

They must be the bucks who had been raiding whites of late, the war party he'd wanted to avoid at all costs. He hurried to the Ovaro and placed a hand over its muzzle to keep it from neighing when the war horses drew nearer. Despite the chill, sweat trickled down his spine. He breathed lightly and stood motionless, watching the approaching warriors.

The Cheyennes were strung out in war-party fashion, in single file with equal spacing between each man and the next. In the lead rode a muscular warrior cradling a rifle in his arms. Three others also carried rifles, the rest bows. All wore buckskin and moccasins, although the leader had somewhere acquired an old army hat now stripped of any insignia and bearing a hole in the front.

Fargo had a good idea who had put the hole there and then appropriated the hat. He cocked the Sharps, waiting expectantly to learn if they would notice the job he'd done of hiding his tracks. They rode at a fast walk, their hardy mounts accustomed to adverse conditions and able to maintain a steady pace for hours on end that few horses bred by whites could duplicate.

He knew a few Cheyennes by sight, but none of those in the war party were familiar. They all had one thing in common; they were young. And they were undoubtedly headstrong and hated all whites, as did many Indians nowadays. All the lies the whites had told, all the deceptions practiced and the treaties broken, had resulted in a widespread resentment of the white culture by those who had inhabited the land long before Columbus set sail for the New World.

Having lived with Indians, Fargo appreciated their anger and understood their reasoning. He also realized there would be no stopping the eventual influx of thousands upon thousands of white settlers, prospectors, and others eager for a new life in an untamed land. Conflict was inevitable, and he had often reflected that one day there would be outright, widespread war.

The Cheyennes were abreast of the stand now, about twenty yards out, still riding westward. The muscular warrior in the lead suddenly drew up and gazed thoughtfully at the trees, and Fargo felt the short hairs at the nape of his neck prickle.

The warrior changed direction and rode toward the stand.

6

Imitating a tree, Fargo held his breath. The leader angled closer to the west end of the stand and seemed to be searching the underbrush for something. At last the Cheyenne stopped, slid to the ground, and said something to his fellows, who had followed and also halted. He stepped into the stand disappearing from Fargo's view.

What was going on?

Skye figured the rest of the war party was no more than fifteen feet from the log on which he'd rested. If one of them should look over a shoulder and spy the brush marks, they would fan out and scour the stand. He could get one, possibly two with the Sharps, and then they would be on him and it would be five to one. Realistically, he knew he wouldn't be able to get them all before they got him.

Where had the leader gone? He probed the brush and thought he saw the warrior hunkered down near a snow-shrouded thicket, but he wasn't certain. Then he noticed the fourth warrior in line. The man had turned and was surveying the sea of white. If his gaze should drop to the log . . .

Fargo removed his hand from the pinto, pressed the Sharps to his right shoulder, and took a bead on the fourth brave. Seconds crawled by. Then the Cheyenne faced front and spoke to the next warrior in line, who laughed.

Shortly thereafter the leader walked out of the trees, hitching at his pants. He tied the draw cord, adjusted a hunting knife nestled in a beaded sheath on his left hip, and swung onto his horse. With a curt word he hastened to the west and the rest dutifully tailed along. Not until they were again dots, only this time on the opposite horizon, did Fargo sigh in relief and lead the Ovaro back to the log. That had been a close one. But now he knew the acting troupe was in little danger from the war party. The Cheyennes were heading west, the company north.

Their paths wouldn't cross and the wagons should reach the trail unmolested.

He let down the hammer on the rifle, replaced it in the scabbard, and climbed into the saddle. Jabbing his spurs lightly, he goaded the stallion into motion. Whether because he was nearer his destination or no longer needed to worry about the war party, the time went by quickly and he soon came to the Solomon River Trail. Covered with snow, it was still easy to locate because it bordered the south fork of the Solomon River on the south side, within yards of the water, and because the passage of countless heavy wagons and horses had formed a wide rut lower than the surrounding ground and the surface of the snow over the rut was lower than that of the surrounding snow by several inches.

There were fresh tracks on the trail, all made by shod horses—which eliminated Indians—heading west.

Fargo crossed his arms over the pommel and leaned down to inspect the prints, surprised anyone was abroad so soon after the blizzard. The nearest way station to the east lay well over sixty miles away. No one could have left it and reached the point where he sat in less than a day and a half, so whoever had passed by had found somewhere to take shelter during the storm and was now hurrying toward the next isolated stop, Miller's Crossing, ninety miles due west. Miller's Crossing was so named because it was situated at a shallow point where those bound for the Rockies crossed over from the south side of the river to the north side and then resumed their travels.

He straightened and reflected. It would take the actors all day to catch up with him. They probably wouldn't show until after dark. Allowing for the difficulties of moving in heavy snow, it would take them nine or ten days to reach Miller's Crossing. Long before then they would run out of wood and food, and they would desperately need his help to stay alive.

The gurgling water drew his attention. Not very deep, it was nearly frozen all the way across. Sluggishly flowing water filled a span of less than a yard.

Fargo saw a few cottonwoods rearing skyward several hundred feet to the west, and he rode over to them and climbed down. This was where he'd wait for the vans to overtake him.

He tied the Ovaro, swiped snow away from the base of the thickest tree, and sat with his back to the trunk. The hours spent in the saddle had fatigued him more than they ordinarily would, no doubt due to his inactivity during the past few days and the blood he'd lost when he'd been attacked. He closed his eyes, intending to rest a short while, and promptly fell asleep.

When next his eyes widened, darkness enveloped the plains. He stood swiftly, angry at himself for sleeping so long. The cold wind moaned on all sides, a stiff wind that would reshape the flat terrain into an unending series of rolling drifts by morning if it persisted. He could see fine white spray shooting into the air at various points.

Overhead, a half-moon dominated the heavens. Stars sparkled against the inky background of infinity. There wasn't a cloud in the sky.

The Ovaro patiently awaited him. He took the reins and walked back along the trail, staring to the south, wondering how soon the wagons would arrive. Allowing for the time it would have taken them to chop wood at the large stand he'd found earlier, they should join him soon. Then he would know if they were following as he'd instructed or whether Frederick had foolishly continued to follow Buffalo Briggs.

Mounting, Fargo rode southward, relying on his unerring instincts to guide him over the featureless landscape. All around, the snow blew and swirled and a fine mist repeatedly struck his face. There were no sounds except for the thud of the Ovaro's hoofs, the stallion's heavy breathing, and the creaking of the saddle.

He thought of Molly. Not Abby. Molly. Which was odd since he'd bedded the blonde beauty and enjoyed it. He should be looking forward to rolling in the sheets with Abby again. Instead, he imagined what it would be like to slip under the covers with Molly. He remembered that look in her eyes when he'd pulled out, and he flattered himself that she felt the same way about him.

He also thought about Buffalo Briggs and the teamsters. If Frederick had listened to him about Briggs, the wagon boss would be fit to be tied. Skye wouldn't be able to turn his back on Grimes or Vangent, either. Which one of them had jumped him? he wondered. He now suspected Grimes, but he still had no idea why they had tried to kill him or what they were up to.

To his surprise, he came on the large vans a mile from the Solomon River Trail. They were hurrying northward, the teams being pushed hard, as he'd directed, and in the pale moonlight he saw a lone rider out ahead of the column.

Buffalo Briggs.

Fargo patted his Colt and rode to intercept them. Briggs spied him and halted. He expected to be greeted with a curse or at the least a surly comment. Instead, sparking astonishment in Fargo, the wagon boss hailed him cordially.

"Howdy, Fargo. We've done just as you wanted. How far is it to the trail?"

Fargo reined up, completely mystified, suspecting a trick. "About a mile," he said warily.

"I can't believe I strayed so far from it," Briggs said. "I seldom lose my way, even in heavy snow. But I guess it happens to the best of us, huh?"

Fargo was at a loss for words. The man's radical change in attitude was inexplicable. A couple of days ago Briggs had tried to draw iron on him. Now Briggs acted as if nothing had happened and they were on friendly terms. Why?

"You don't know how glad I am you came along," Briggs said sincerely. "I would have realized my mistake sooner or later, but you've saved us a lot of time." He paused and shifted uncomfortably. "And if you'll let me, I'd like to apologize for all the trouble I gave you. I'm naturally short-tempered, and I didn't like you horning in and accusing me of being a yack."

Flabbergasted, Fargo sat mute.

"I'd be happy if you'd ride with us at least to Miller's Crossing. Denver, if you want. But I could use your help getting these folks to the crossing."

"I plan to stick with the train for quite a spell," Fargo said.

"Good." Briggs smiled and gazed upward. "At least we have a bit of moonlight to show the way. These folks are tired and they'll be glad to reach the trail. You should have seen them work cutting down trees and gathering the wood we needed. Took them under an hour with everyone pitching in."

"Did you see the war party?" Fargo asked.

Briggs leaned forward. "No, but I saw the tracks. Didn't mention anything to Federick or the others because I didn't want to worry them. Besides, those Injuns were heading west. Did you see them?"

"Yep. Seven Cheyennes out for scalps. I figure it's the same bunch that hit a wagon train a couple of weeks ago."

"Hopefully they're miles away by now."

The wagons were nearly on them. Grimes was driving the lead van and he didn't bother to acknowledge Fargo's presence.

"A mile or so!" Briggs called out to him.

Grimes gave a little wave to indicate he'd heard, then forged on.

"Don't pay no attention to him," Briggs said. "He's still mad over the beating you gave him this morning."

Fargo rode back along the line of wagons, feeling bewildered. Had he missed something? Why was Briggs being so nice? Could it be a trick to get him to lower his guard? Yet the man's gratitude had certainly seemed genuine.

He looped up behind Molly's wagon and knocked on the door. A moment later it opened, only Chelsea stood framed in the doorway.

"Why, hello there, handsome. We've missed you."

Molly appeared behind her. "Skye! Did you have any problems?"

"Nothing major. How did the day go?"

"The morning was bad. Tom Frederick gave Briggs a tongue-lashing that everyone in the company heard. Then we started out on your trail. By the time we stopped to chop wood, Briggs was a new man. He apologized to Frederick and was friendly to everyone. Frankly, I didn't know what to make of it."

"Makes two of us," Fargo said. "Listen, we'll be at the trail soon and we'll stop for the night. I'd sure like an invite for some coffee."

"How about some stew, too?" Molly asked.

"Thanks," Fargo said, and swung the stallion toward the rear of the column, critically regarding every horse and noting the condition of each wagon. The team animals were fatigued but holding up well. There were ample oats for feed, enough to last perhaps five of the ten days it would take to reach Miller's Crossing. After that, with the sweet buffalo grass buried under the heavy mantle of snow, uncovering forage would be time-consuming but not impossible. Water, since the Solomon River was close by, would be easily attainable. The main threats to the health of the animals were the cold and the snow. It took a lot out of man or beasts to plow through deep snow hours on end. The strength flagged, the body temperature dropped, and before either man or beasts knew it they were too weak to go on.

The wagons were in excellent shape. The wood panels were in prime condition, the paint fresh and bright. Skye figured Frederick had purchased them shortly before leaving Chicago. He'd seen such vans before, but they were far from common. Snake-oil salesmen used them on occasion, and itinerant preachers did sometimes. Long-bodied and low to the ground, they could travel at a decent clip over flat land but were next to useless in really rugged country. These were so low their undercarriages barely cleared the snow. Conestogas and prairie schooners were better fitted to plains travel, but their canvas tops provided scant protection from the elements.

Fargo made a complete circuit of the wagon train and returned to the head of the column. The wind continued to blow, the snow contined to drift, and he dreaded the difficulty they would face come morning. High drifts would thwart the vans as effectively as brick walls.

Buffalo Briggs, still acting as friendly as they came, turned and nodded at the big man. "We're making good time."

"Yep," Fargo responded laconically. No way did he trust the man, and he wasn't about to act as if their fences had been mended when his instincts told him the man was an enemy.

"Tell the truth, I can't wait to get these folks to Miller's Crossing."

"You'll only be about halfway to the Rockies. The worst land is past the crossing, where it's drier and there's less game and more Indians on the prowl."

"I know," Briggs said, not sounding worried in the least. "But I'll take it one step at a time, and Miller's Crossing is the big step as far as I'm concerned."

Fargo pursed his lips. The man was doing it again, was making no sense. The stretch past Miller's Crossing would be sheer hell, yet the wagon boss was completely unruffled by the prospect of the grueling trip. Why?

They rode in silence until they came to the Solomon River Trail. Briggs motioned for the wagons to pull onto the trail and face westward, then called a halt. The teams were taken out of their harnesses, fed, and tethered. Briggs gave Grimes the first guard shift.

Despite himself, Fargo had to admit the man was doing everything right. He bedded down the Ovaro, then lugged his gear and saddle to Frederick's wagon. Inside were the head of the troupe, Kevin O'Casey, and Pete.

"We looked out the window and saw you earlier, boyo," the Irishman said. "Glad you're still with us."

Fargo arranged his gear as before and walked over to the stove. A pot of coffee rested on the griddle, the aroma tantalizing. His mouth watered.

"Help yourself to a cup, Mr. Fargo," Frederick said. "And then, if you would, I'd like a few words with you."

Skye only took half a cup. He preferred to wait to slake his thirst until he got to Molly's wagon. Rotating, he pressed the tin cup to his lips and slowly savored the delicious hot liquid. "What about?"

"Kevin has informed me of the disputes you've had with Buffalo Briggs since your arrival," Frederick said. "I've also given considerable thought to what you told me this morning. I now have grave doubts about Briggs and his abilities as a wagon boss. What do you think of the idea of firing him right now?"

"I'd hold off," Fargo said. "You're on the trail, so there's little chance he can get you lost again. And you might need him over the next week or so."

"Will you be staying with us?"

"For as long as I need to," Fargo said, swallowing more coffee and smiling as intense warmth spread from his mouth, down his throat, and into his chest.

Frederick ran a hand through his long hair. "I'm particularly concerned by Schweer's death. If, as you believe, Indians were not responsible, then that means someone else on the train must be the culprit.''

"Looks that way," Fargo said.

"Well, I doubt whether it was one of my troupe. Briggs, possibly. Grimes and Vangent, maybe. But not one of my people. As I mentioned before, there isn't a member of the company who I don't know as well as I do my own brother and sister. None of them are killers. They've all been with us a long time.''

"Except Hulbert and Torrez," Kevin corrected. "They've only been with us about a year." He paused. "Come to think of it, Bill Schweer had been with us for less than a year also.''

"What about the other man, Jack Wehner?" Fargo inquired, his interest aroused. Could there be some connection between the deaths and the length of time the victims had been with the troupe?

Frederick answered. "Jack was with us for nine years last August. He must have been careless and slipped. Such a fine man! And only the day before we departed Chicago.''

"Did you get anyone to replace him?" Fargo asked.

"Pete and two of the other men can handle the few props we're using on this trip," Frederick said. "Once we're back in the Windy City, I'll hire a new prop man.''

Fargo was disappointed his hunch had not panned out. He finished off the coffee, adjusted his hat, and headed for the door.

"Where are you going now?" Pete asked.

"Not that it's any of your business, but I've been invited to supper. I'll be at Molly's wagon if you need me.''

O'Casey chuckled. "You know, boyo, you remind me of me when I was young. Makes me pine for the grand old days when the women swooned over me.''

Pete snorted. "The only woman who ever swooned over you was your mother, and that was when she fainted in childbirth.''

The Irishman uttered a string of colorful curses, and Fargo stepped into the night grinning. The camp was quiet. Some of the troupe had turned out to stretch their legs when the vans stopped, but now they were all snug inside where it was warm, preparing or eating their evening meals. Smoke wafted from the stovepipes at the front of the wagons and the scents of cooking hung heavy in the brisk air. Someone was frying bacon. It made his stomach growl.

He walked toward Molly's van, gazing idly at the horses, then halted. Grimes was nowhere in sight. Not that he cared about the hardcase, but he did care about the horses. Without the stock, the acting company would be in great jeopardy. With a Cheyenne war party in the area, the horses must be watched at all times.

Suspecting the teamster was shirking his duty and resting instead of watching, Fargo moved to the string, his boots swishing the deep snow aside, and halted. A vague feeling in his gut prompted him to move his coat back so he would have instant access to the Colt. Something was wrong. He didn't know what, but he knew as sure as he breathed that all was not well.

Then he saw the tracks, boot tracks leading along the front of the tethered animals and around the far end. He followed them, knowing Grimes had made them. The cottonwoods where he had slept were close by, perhaps twenty feet to the rear of the string. They were bare of vegetation, as stark as death itself.

Fargo came around the end of the string, his eyes locked on the ground, and saw the boot heels. Then the boots and the legs and the entire body lying facedown with a dark stain spreading out from the neck. It was Grimes, dead. Fargo's hand closed on the Colt, and as it did he heard the soft rush of moccasin-covered feet behind him, a hair before a heavy body slammed into his back.

7

In a way, the previous attack saved Fargo's life now. Having dealt with almost the selfsame situation a couple of days ago, his reflexes were a shade sharper than they might have been otherwise. At the instant his attacker rammed him in the back, Fargo threw himself to the right, trying to avoid being pinned. An iron hand had gripped his hair at the impact, knocking off his hat as it did, and the attacker yanked on his head as they fell, trying to tilt his neck, to expose it for a throat slash. By throwing himself to one side, Fargo caused the hasty grip on his hair to loosen and the attacker to fall to the left.

Skye scrambled into a crouch. Already his assailant was up and charging, and he wasn't at all startled to discover it was a stocky Cheyenne wielding a hunting knife. He backpedaled to evade a swing and clawed for the Colt, but the warrior darted in close and stabbed at his gun hand. The tip of the blade fanned his skin.

Smooth movement was impeded by the snow. Fargo's legs shuffled awkwardly and his boots slipped. He tottered rearward, lashing a fist at the Cheyenne when the man tried to quickly end their fight. And then, out of the corner of his eye, he detected a second Cheyenne a dozen feet away standing upright and drawing back on a bowstring. He realized the first warrior was keeping him occupied so the second could finish him off. And he frustrated their ploy by letting himself fall, his right hand swooping to the Colt.

A shaft streaked out of the darkness, whizzing within inches of Fargo's torso as he went down. Had he been standing he would have been pierced. But the arrow missed and he wound up flat on his back with the .44 leaping free and flaming lead as the first Cheyenne leaped. The slug took the brave high in the chest and flipped him clean over.

Rolling onto his side, Fargo extended the big revolver and

banged off two shots at the bowman. The man staggered, yet was able to release another arrow, and this one flew true. Fargo felt a searing pain in his left shoulder as the shaft hit home. Grimly, he surged to a knee and thumbed off another shot, and this one dropped the buck where he stood.

Fargo glanced at the first Cheyenne, then the second, but neither moved. From behind the cottonwoods came the sudden drumming of hoofs. "Damn!" he fumed, and rose. He raced to the trees. Galloping to the southwest was a third Cheyenne, who was leading the two horses of his slain companions. Fargo couldn't let him get away. He elevated the Colt, wishing he had the Sharps, and took careful aim. The Cheyenne, though, rode hunched low over the horse, a difficult target under any circumstances. Skye cocked the hammer, steadied the .44, and fired.

Nothing happened. The Cheyenne kept riding. The two riderless horses never slowed.

He'd missed.

Fargo didn't waste another shot. The Cheyenne was a shadowy shape in the night, diminishing rapidly, impossible to hit. He sighed and walked back to where the dead warriors lay.

Shafts of light speared from the rear of each wagon as the doors were thrown open and the startled actors and actresses burst out. They spilled onto the snow and gazed around in confusion until someone spied Fargo, shouted, and a mad rush brought them over.

Skye began reloading the Colt. Never leave a gun empty was the first rule of survival west of the Mississippi, a rule he never violated. He pondered how the attack would effect the troupe, what it meant in terms of reaching Miller's Crossing safely, and he didn't like his conclusions. There were voices all around him, but he paid no attention until someone stepped in front of him.

"How many was there?"

Fargo looked up as he holstered the revolver. It was Briggs. Near him stood Frederick and Kevin O'Casey, both gaping at the dead Indians. "Three," he said.

Briggs looked around. "One got away?"

"Afraid so."

"That's bad news."

"You're telling me," Fargo said. Someone gently touched his right arm and he glanced around to discover Molly, anxiety etching her countenance.

"You seem to be making a habit out of getting yourself hurt," she said softly, nodding at his left shoulder.

Fargo had nearly forgotten about the arrow. The barbed tip jutted out the back of his coat while most of the shaft and the feathers stuck out the front. He felt blood trickling down his skin but little pain.

"You killed two of them," Tom Frederick said. "Does this mean the rest will leave us alone?"

"No," Fargo said. "I don't think these three were part of the war party I saw earlier. I think they were riding to join it when they spotted the wagons and trailed us here. They were fixing to steal our horses. Grimes must have heard them and been killed."

"But they know we aren't to be trifled with," Frederick said, using typically illogical Eastern logic and demonstrating his complete ignorance of Indians. "The one who got away will tell the others and they'll steer clear of us."

"He'll tell the others, all right," Fargo agreed, "but they'll make tracks to catch us before we can reach Miller's Crossing. They'll want to pay us back for these deaths and they won't stop until they draw blood."

"What do we do?" Frederick asked, his tone strained, ignoring Buffalo Briggs. "Should we arm all the men and post guards around the wagons until dawn?"

"That won't be necessary," Fargo answered. "The brave who rode off won't overtake the war party until sometime tomorrow afternoon or evening, even if he rides without stopping. It will take them another day or more to catch us. Three days from now is when you can start worrying."

"What if we send a rider on ahead to Miller's Crossing for help?" Frederick asked.

"There's no one there who could lend a hand," Fargo said. "Old Jacob Miller owns it. He and his wife have lived there for more years than I can remember."

"There might be other travelers staying there," Frederick said.

"Maybe so, but I don't think they'd be all too eager to tangle with a band of bloodthirsty Cheyennes," Fargo countered. "Besides, whoever we sent couldn't possibly get back before the war party hits us."

"And we're too far from Fort Leavenworth to send someone there," Buffalo Briggs said.

"You folks are on your own," Fargo said, and saw apprehension spread rampant among them. They shared worried expressions and fidgeted nervously. "For now, bury the bodies. We'll plan how to deal with the war party tomorrow."

"What about Grimes?" Pete asked. "Should we wrap him in a canvas ground sheet and take him with us? He's a white man. He deserves a proper burial."

"If you take him along, you'll be stuffing blanket wads up your noses in a couple of days," Fargo said. "No, you'd better collect his personal effects and plant him here. You can always contact his kin later." Weariness suddenly assailed him and he turned, making for Molly's wagon. The many hours in the saddle and the aggravating wound in his side had taken their toll. He was talked out. He wanted food and rest and out of the cold.

Molly was at his side. "Does the arm hurt?" she asked in a small voice.

"Not much," Fargo said. He couldn't tell without removing his coat, but he doubted the new wound was very serious. At the van he opened the door for her, then went in. The heady odor of simmering stew stopped him in his tracks. "I'm starved," he commented, pleased to find they were alone. Chelsea and Abby were outside with the rest, and he figured they would spend time discussing what had just happened. Good.

"I'll feed you after we tend your arm," Molly said, going to a closet in the far corner. "I stored the bag in here," she said, and removed the brown leather valise.

Sitting on a bunk, Skye stripped off his skeepskin coat. The arrow came with it. On examination, he found the shaft had penetrated the heavy material, sliced his shirt and nicked his arm, and then emerged out the back of the sleeve. He'd bled some, but not enough to require a bandage.

Molly stared at the arrow as he snapped it near the barbed

head and removed it from his coat. "You were lucky, Skye Fargo," she said. "Now take off your shirt."

"It's just a scratch."

"Please. You don't want it to become infected, do you?"

Eager to eat, he dutifully removed the shirt and sat still so she could wash the nick. He noticed how her cheeks flushed when she gazed at his hard, muscular chest, and saw her lick her lips when he flexed his powerful arms.

"Sit still, will you?"

"Sorry, ma'am."

For such a little scratch, it took Molly a long time to wipe it clean to her satisfaction and apply a dab of ointment. She gently, and apparently unconsciously, traced a finger down his forearm as she finished. Then she put the medical supplies back into the valise and carried the valise to the closet.

"How about that stew?" Fargo asked.

Molly was quiet as she dished out a heaping bowl of the steaming stew and brought it over. "Hope you like this. Vangent shot a rabbit today when we were stopped to chop wood. He gave most of it to Abby and she let me use it in the stew."

"Nice of him."

"I think Vangent has a crush on her. Most men do. But she doesn't even know he exists."

"Figures," Skye said, taking a mouthful of the delicious meal. He rolled the broth in his mouth and closed his eyes. "You make the best stew I've ever ate."

"You only say that because you're half starved," Molly said, grinning.

"I say it because it's true," Fargo responded. He'd made no effort to don his shirt, and her eyes were constantly straying to his chest. He returned the compliment, imagining how she would look without her dress.

Stepping to the bunk across from the one on which he sat, Molly sank down and rested her chin in her hands. "Abby has been bragging about her conquest of you," she stated.

The unexpected declaration caught Fargo flat-footed. He paused, his spoon part way to his mouth, wondering why she had brought it up. "Oh?"

"Don't bother denying it," Molly said without reproach.

"We all know what happened in here the other day. And we all know how Abby loves to brag. She's not the shy sort, as I guess you've noticed."

Fargo took another spoonful of stew. There were times when a man, if he had any brains at all, knew to keep his mouth shut and his ears open. This, without a doubt, was one of those times.

"I didn't want to believe her," Molly said. "It upset me immensely, and it took me a while to admit to myself why I was upset." She took a breath. "I like you, Skye Fargo. Like you a lot. You turn my insides to butter, and no man has done that since my husband passed away a year ago."

"I'm flattered," Fargo said.

"Let me say the rest. I like you, but I know your kind as well as I know Abby's. You're not the marrying kind, and no woman will ever get you to settle down until you're good and ready."

Skye ate more stew. She had him pegged, sure enough. But what was her point?

"I like you and I want you, but I've never slept with any man except my husband and I don't know if I could with you when I know nothing will come of it in the long run," Molly said in a rush. Then she bowed her head, disturbed.

"No one can force you to do anything you're not inclined to," Fargo said. "As for us, if something happens, let it happen naturally. I'm not about to try and force myself on you."

"I know. I didn't mean—"

"You're not Abby. She shucks her clothes at the drop of a hat, and the odds of her making some man a fine wife one day are as slim as finding gold in a chamber pot. You, on the other hand, will find the gent you want and raise a fine family."

Molly brightened. "What a nice thing to say," she exclaimed, and came over. Before he quite knew what to expect, she kissed him hard full on the lips, hard but fleetingly, a kiss that promised so much more if she should ever decide it was right. Then she took his bowl and went to the stove for a second helping of stew.

Skye Fargo regarded her thoughtfully. In his wide, unending travels he'd met a lot of women and known more than his share intimately. He'd bedded more fallen doves than any ten cow men, slept with more Indian women than any ten mountain men.

Not that he always planned it that way. He was a ruggedly handsome hombre—or so all the ladies told him—and they seemed to sense a quality about him that they admired. And wanted. Some men were like that. Women flocked to them like kids to candy. Other men couldn't get a woman interested no matter how hard they tried.

And Skye liked being popular with the women. He took their attention in stride and made the most of it. If a lovely wanted him, he rarely turned her down. In his estimation, only priests, monks, and eunuchs needed to abstain, and he had his doubts about eunuchs. He was a healthy, virile man, as randy as any stallion, and he intended to fully satisfy his craving every chance he got.

Women like Molly, though, sometimes gave him pause. They were the quiet ones, the women who had been reared by strict parents to be morally proper and never give themselves to a man without a commitment from him. Yet these women wanted men as much as the fallen doves did. They enjoyed men just as much. Once these women overcame the hurdle of their upbringing, they became wildcats in bed. And Fargo had a hunch Molly would be one of the wildest. He could wait for her to come around.

She came back bearing the steaming bowl. "Here you go."

He took the bowl, placed it beside him, and lifted his shirt to put it on. As his arms rose, Molly stepped between them and gave him another kiss. Only this one was the kiss to end all kisses, her full lips molded to his, her tongue lashing his in a frenzy of arousal. He felt her body press against his, felt her breasts mash into his skin, and felt his manhood spring to attention.

Molly moaned deep in her throat.

Fargo ran his hands over her buttocks, then up to the small of her slender back. Every inch of her skin radiated intense heat. He slid his hands higher, going for her breasts, when there came a scratching noise at the door and she abruptly stepped backward, flustered but striving to compose herself.

A gust of cold air struck Fargo as he turned. Just climbing in were Chelsea, Abby, and Tom Frederick.

Abby put her hands on her hips and smirked. "Well, what

have we here? I hope we're not interrupting anything important?''

"Not at all," Molly said, her voice constricted and husky. "I was just cleaning Skye's wound."

"Sure you were, darling," Abby said sarcastically.

"That'll be enough out of you, missy," Chelsea chided her. "What these two were doing is none of our business."

Fargo resumed donning his shirt as Frederick walked over to the bunk. "Something on your mind?"

"Buffalo Briggs has set up a guard schedule for tonight. Vangent will pull the first shift, then Briggs, then two of our men will take turns until morning. Does that sound adequate to you?"

"We shouldn't have trouble tonight," Fargo said, tucking the shirt into his pants and adjusting his gunbelt.

"I don't trust Briggs anymore," Frederick said. "You told me not to fire him, but how about if I tell him you're now in charge and he's second-in-command? How would that be?"

"No need. I'll stay with you to the crossing, and if he does anything suspicious I'll let you know."

"Fair enough," Frederick said, his features haggard. The strain of the trip, his illness, and now these latest difficulties were taking a heavy toll. He was an actor, not a laborer. The hardest physical work he usually did consisted of moving props around in the course of a play. He was accustomed to reciting and voicing lines in a heated theater, not to the Plains in the dead of winter. His face was tinged with regret as he walked toward the door. "I should never have organized this tour. It's become a living hell." Out he went, his shoulders drooping.

"Tom never could see the bright side of things," Abby said, removing her coat. Then she blinked, then laughed. "What the hell am I talking about? There is no bright side to this mess we're in."

"A lady doesn't use profanity," Chelsea said sternly.

"Oh, please," Abby said. "Honestly, sometimes you act just like my mother."

"Whom I'll wager you didn't listen to a day of your life," Chelsea responded.

Fargo expected Abby to become angry. Instead, the vixen laughed and nodded.

"Now that you mention it, I didn't. A girl has so much more fun that way."

The conversation became a discussion of Abby's upbringing, and she went on at length about her sexual escapades, completely uninhibited. Fargo ate and listened, noticing Molly hardly put in a word. Several times she glanced at him and blushed. When he'd finished the stew, he handed over the bowl and rose. "Time for me to catch some shut-eye."

"You could stay the night," Abby suggested, the devil in her eyes. "We have a spare bunk."

"A man doesn't poke his head in a bear trap unless he wants to lose it," Fargo said, and shrugged into his coat. He nodded at Chelsea and Molly, then departed. The camp was quiet again, with most of the company inside their wagons. Vangent stood near the horses, and near the cottonwoods were four men digging furiously. Fargo knew they wouldn't be able to dig very deep because of the frozen ground, but they'd manage shallow graves and that would be enough to foil the scavengers. His legs moved tiredly as he stepped into his own wagon. Frederick was lying down. Pete and the Irishman were by the stove, drinking coffee.

"Fargo," Pete said without preliminaries. "What will this war party do when they find us? Pick us off one by one?"

"Depends on the brave running the show. They might content themselves with swooping down on us when we least expect it and shooting two or three. Or they might want to capture a few of us to torture."

"Torture?" Pete repeated, the blood rushing from his face.

"Some Indians like to torture whites. It's not that the Indians are cruel by nature. They just admire bravery above all else, and when they torture someone it's a test of bravery. If the man doesn't cry out or scream, they'll put him out of his misery quickly because they respect him."

"And if he does cry out?"

Fargo shrugged. "Then they'll skin him alive or cut off his fingers or do any of the thousand and one things they think up. If he's a coward, he doesn't deserve a quick death."

"How barbaric," O'Casey said.

"To your way of thinking," Fargo said, hanging up his coat. He took the Sharps to his bunk and began cleaning it. His Colt would get the same treatment.

"Surely you don't approve?" Kevin said.

"It's not for me to judge folks," Fargo answered. "If I did, I sure wouldn't blame the Indians. They've been lied to by us every time we open our mouths. We sign treaties one day and break them the next. Each year more and more settlers are heading west. One day we'll push the Indians right off their land, and some of them know it. They're the ones who like to carve us into little pieces."

O'Casey cocked his head. "And you stay out here where any day they could do you in? Why?"

Fargo looked up. "I like being free," he said simply.

The Irishman scratched his chin, then clucked like a bewildered hen. "If you don't mind my saying so, you're a strange one, boyo. Many back East would feel the same way I do."

"Doesn't matter to me how other folks feel. Only one thing is important where I'm concerned."

"What's that?"

"I'm alive."

8

The next day was sheer torture.

Fargo awoke before dawn, washed his chest and face, using a pail of water and a washbowl situated in a corner of the van, then combed his hair and stepped outside to greet the dawn. The wind knifed into him the instant the door opened, and he bundled his coat tighter about him.

One glance at the sea of snow confirmed his worst fears. During the night the strong winds had reshaped the landscape, turning the essentially flat white blanket into an ocean of rolling drifts of varying heights stretching for as far as the eye could see. Many of the drifts were only two to three feet high, while others crested at a good six feet or more. The snowy waves crisscrossed the Solomon River Trail at close intervals, one after the other, on and on and on, presenting an unending series of obstacles that must be overcome before the wagons could make headway.

Skye Fargo trudged through the snow to check on the horses and found the actor who was pulling the last guard shift dozing on his feet. He gave the man a nudge, and when the actor jumped and fumbled with his rifle, he smiled and said, "Rise and shine, mister. We'll be leaving soon." He turned toward the feed wagon. "And if you pull this stunt three days from now, you might wake up with your throat cut from ear to ear."

"Sorry," the man blurted sheepishly.

"It's your life," Fargo told him. At the door to Brigg's wagon he paused and knocked. Now that they were the best of friends—and he smiled wryly at the thought—he didn't want to get on the wrong side of the wagon boss. At least not yet, not until the acting company was safe at Miller's Crossing. He didn't know if Briggs or the others would be up, but young Tyler answered the door immediately.

"Mr. Fargo! You're up early. Come on in."

Fargo found Briggs and Vangent seated on their respective bunks, drinking coffee. He helped himself to a feed bag and filled it from the bin.

"How's it look out there?" Briggs asked.

"Let me put it this way," Fargo said. "Frederick will get his money's worth out of you today."

"Damn."

Fargo departed, fitted the feed bag to the Ovaro, and returned to his own wagon. Kevin O'Casey had risen and was fixing coffee. "Smells good," Skye said.

"My sainted mother made the best coffee in all of Ireland," Kevin said with a trace of melancholy. "Picked up the knack from her, I think, because my dear father couldn't make coffee if his life depended on it."

"Miss Ireland much?"

"Now and then," O'Casey answered, "but not as much as you might think. I was always a traveling man. Before I came to America, I went back and forth across Europe twice." He leaned over the coffeepot. "What's taking this brew so long to heat up today?"

"How much extra rope and harness do you have?" Fargo asked, dusting snow off the bottom of his pants.

"Plenty," O'Casey said. "It's stored in the last wagon. Briggs told us we might run into heavy snow and should have a lot handy, so Tom went out and bought all he could."

Briggs said that? Fargo's brow furrowed in contemplation. The man wasn't completely incompetent, then. It added to the mystery of who Buffalo Briggs really was and what his intentions were.

"Why do you want to know about the rope, boyo?"

"The trail is drifted shut. We'll need it to get these heavy wagons through the drifts. By tonight every man in this outfit will be so tired he won't be able to lift an arm."

"You sound as if you've done this sort of thing before," Kevin commented.

"I've led a few wagon trains in my time," Fargo said. "Though I usually don't try to take one across the plains in the middle of winter."

"Lots of folks do it, I hear."

"And lots of folks die on the way."

They drank their coffee in silence. Frederick and Pete awakened and were informed about the situation, and then Fargo went out and saddled the Ovaro. The big horse was eager to hit the trail, to get its blood flowing so it would feel warm again after the long, cold night. Its breath formed into cloudlike puffs and it stamped its great hoofs as Fargo lowered the stirrup after cinching up.

He stepped into the saddle and made a complete circuit of the wagons. He found the tracks made by the fleeing buck, and those the two warriors had made while creeping from the cottonwoods to the horses, but no others. Satisfied, he rode westward, skirting the higher drifts where possible. To his right the Solomon River was nearly frozen solid. If it got any colder they would have to use axes to chop chunks of ice and then boil the ice on the stove.

Nothing stirred in the milky vastness, not so much as a sparrow. Even the birds knew enough not to fly in such weather unless it was absolutely necessary. The small varmints were snug in their burrows. And any deer in the area were resting in stands of trees or in the snow-covered thickets along the river. The buffalo were now farther south. Once, there would have been large herds in the vicinity of the Solomon, but those herds had been reduced substantially by the many white men flocking to the Rockies.

Skye rode a mile, then swept back in a loop to the wagons. Every member of the troupe appeared to be up, and the men were busy at work under Briggs's direction. In order to get each van into motion by breaking the iron grip of the ice under the wheels, they had to hook two teams to each wagon, strain and puff until the wagon was rocked loose, and then repeat the procedure with the next van. It took over an hour of back-busting labor.

Finally they got underway. Briggs, Vangent, and two of the troupe rode in front of the train, using their mounts to break through the steeper drifts and make it easier for the wagons. The going was slow, aggravatingly so. By noon the wagons had covered a mere four miles.

Fargo ate with Molly. She was glad to see him and talked

about her childhood, how she had been raised by her mother after her father died when she was six. How she'd always liked singing and dressing up and becoming an actress was a dream come true. Abby and Chelsea were also in the wagon, preventing Fargo from doing more than talk. He got done eating and hit the trail again, helping out wherever he was needed, goading on a stuck team one moment, breaking a path through the drifts the next. By nightfall he was so exhausted he rolled into his bunk with all his clothes on.

And so it went for the next two days.

The horses surged and wheezed while the drivers cracked their whips and cursed, and slowly but surely the wagon train inched westward. Behind them their tracks seemed to stretch all the way to the Mississippi. They saw no one and game was exceedingly scarce.

On the morning of the third day Fargo spied a wide stand of trees to the south and went to investigate. There were fresh rabbit tracks under a snow-crowned bush, so he pulled out the Sharps and made a sweep, going from tree to tree and poking into every bit of undergrowth until he spooked it. Actually, he spooked two, and he shot both as they were racing away in stark panic, putting a slug in the head of each.

After tying the rabbits together with a strip of rawhide and slinging them over his saddle horn, Fargo made a circuit of the countryside to the southwest. If the Cheyenne were coming, they would come from that direction. He found no hoof prints and saw no one.

Still, he knew they were on their way.

Darkness had descended by the time he rejoined the train. The wagons had been halted for the night at a bend in the river and were strung out in a line. He rode up to where Briggs and Vangent were tethering the stock and slid to the ground. "You should have put the wagons in a circle," he said.

Buffalo Briggs turned, anger flaring for all of two seconds. Then he pursed his lips and pondered. "Yep. I see your point. Reckon I made a mistake. Want me to hitch up the teams and do it?"

"No," Fargo said, seeing how tired the horses were. They would balk at being put back in harness and would give the drivers a hell of a time. Better to let them have their well-deserved rest and not make the same blunder the next night. "But post two guards instead of one and have them keep walking around the wagons."

"I'm so sick of pulling guard duty," Vangent grumbled, and glared at the Trailsman. "How come you never do? You too good to be bothered?"

"Say when and I'll be here," Fargo told him, irritated by the teamster's taunting.

"How about the second shift, right after mine?" Buffalo Briggs said. "Kevin O'Casey will be on with you."

"Fine." Fargo tramped to the wagon, the rabbits in his right hand, the Sharps in his left. He gave the game to Pete, who was preparing their supper, and went back outside to tend to the Ovaro. Repeatedly he scanned the unending snowfield, but saw nothing to arouse alarm.

Once on his bunk with his coat off, Fargo wiped down both the Colt and the Sharps and made certain each was loaded. He was sharpening the toothpick when Pete walked over bearing a small plate of rabbit.

"Might be tonight, huh?"

"Might be," Fargo acknowledged, staring at the small portion.

Pete noticed. "Sorry, it's not much but we're low on grub. I'm going to share the rabbit with some of those in the other wagons."

"Tomorrow I'll try to find deer," Fargo promised. He forked the meat into his mouth slowly, relishing each morsel, his stomach doing flip-flops. As hungry as he was, he could have eaten a steer. Raw.

"I'm pulling a guard shift tonight," Kevin said, trying hard to conceal his nervousness. He lifted a rifle. "I'm not a marksman, but I'll do the best I can."

"We're on the same shift," Fargo informed him, and suppressed a laugh when the Irishman's features rippled in heartfelt relief.

"The two of us together, boyo? Why, we'll murder those heathens if they show their red hides."

"They might not even come," Tom Frederick said. "Isn't that right, Fargo?"

"They'll come, all right," Fargo said, his mouth crammed with rabbit. "Maybe not tonight, but they'll come. And when they do, we'd better be prepared."

"We are," Frederick stated. "I've passed out all of our firearms and issued ammunition. Every man will be on his toes from now until we reach Miller's Crossing. You said yourself there were only seven braves in that war party. They'll think twice before they hit a wagon train our size."

"There will be eight counting the one who got away the other night," Fargo reminded him. "And Indians don't care much about odds when they're on the warpath."

Frederick digested the information, then frowned. "I must have been crazy to start the tour at this time of year. What was going through my head?"

"All the money you could make," Kevin said. "In the spring and summer we'd have a lot of competition from other troupes. Our receipts wouldn't be as high. This way, we stand to make more money."

"If we're alive to collect it," Pete said glumly.

There was no moon. A myriad of stars afforded a fascinating celestial spectacle. The wind had died down, except for a periodic whisper. All was quiet and tranquil.

"I've never been so scared in my life," Kevin O'Casey said, holding the rifle as if ready to blast away at every shadow. "How can you stand there so calm and collected?"

"Practice," Fargo said. They had just relieved the two sentries before them and were standing near the middle of the train, not far from the tethered stock.

"You're the expert at this. What do we do?"

"Separate and walk around the wagons. Keep close to them and never stand still. Stay in the darkest shadows and stop often to look and listen. If you see something move out there, shoot."

"I'll probably miss."

"The Cheyennes don't know you're a terrible shot. They'll go to ground and give me time to come lend a hand."

"Just don't dawdle, boyo," the Irishman said, walking eastward. "Oh, what I wouldn't give to be back in sunny Ireland right this minute, standing on the banks of the beautiful Shannon

River with a lovely lass." He muttered under his breath and was soon lost in the gloom.

Fargo ambled westward, staying close to the wagons, where he could take prompt cover underneath should the Cheyennes open fire. The temperature hadn't plummeted as far as on previous nights, and although it was cold it wasn't uncomfortable. He walked all the way around, passing Kevin en route, and started his second circuit.

To the south a coyote yipped.

Halting, Skye listened intently. Had it been a real coyote or a Cheyenne? Some warriors were so adept at mimicking animals, there was no way to tell them apart. He slid behind the nearest wagon and waited for the call to be repeated, but a minute went by and only the wind made sounds.

"Fargo?" It was Kevin, rifle at the ready, glancing anxiously right and left. "Where the hell are you?"

"Here," Fargo whispered as he reached out and pulled the Irishman into the shelter of the wagon. "Keep quiet. We may have company."

"Oh, Lord."

Something moved far out on the snow. Skye tensed and cocked the Sharps, heard Kevin gasp, and edged to the corner to get a wider view of the plain. There were no trees, no vegetation whatsoever. How could the Cheyenne hope to get close enough without any cover?

"Are they here?" Kevin whispered.

"Shhh," Fargo said. A flicker of motion off to the left and over thirty yards from the wagons made his lake-blue eyes narrow. Was it a coyote or a Cheyenne? A coyote might be curious and investigate.

"Uh, boyo?" Kevin said softly but urgently.

"Quiet," Fargo directed.

"But this is important. I think there's some of those Cheyennes sneaking up on us on this side."

Shifting, Fargo glanced at the river, doubtful the Indians would try such an approach. Then he reminded himself that the river was practically frozen and it would be easy for them to slip across, and at the same instant he spied an indistinct form, an inky spider scuttling across the light-colored ice not twenty yards off. "Crawl under the wagons until you reach Briggs's. Let him know the war party is about to attack."

"Oh, Lord. Oh, Lord. Oh, Lord," Kevin said, dropping to his hands and knees and scooting under the van.

Fargo was surprised the Cheyennes had decided to hit the wagon train at night. Indians rarely raided after dark, although the Apaches would do so on occasion. Some tribes believed that if a warrior was slain at night, he was doomed to wander as a shiftless spirit. For whatever reason, these Cheyenne were willing to violate the taboo.

The warrior crossing the ice was nearest, so Skye cocked the big rifle, sighted carefully on the darting figure, and waited until the brave reached the edge of the river before squeezing the trigger. The Sharps thundered, and from the Cheyenne came a squeal of pain.

As if the shot were a signal for the other warriors, guns blossomed up and down the line and fierce war whoops rent the air. Only one of the rounds came close to Skye, smacking into the van within inches of his head. He abruptly realized that most of the shots were being directed *at the wagons*! The Cheyennes were trying to inflict as many casualties as they could. And while the wooden sides of the vans were thick, they weren't thick enough to prevent all the shots from penetrating.

Fargo fed in another cartridge and aimed as best he could at a fleeting shadow to the south. He fired hastily and the brave went to ground, suddenly as invisible as if the snow had swallowed him up. Somewhere up the line another rifle boomed, indicating another defender was fighting back. He inserted a third cartridge and lifted the rifle, but before he could take a bead he heard a sound that made him throw caution to the wind and commit an extremely rash act.

From Molly's wagon arose a terrified shriek, then the muffled yell of someone shouting, "I've been hit! I'm hit!"

Instantly Fargo raced toward the van, exposing himself with the first stride, and to the north a rifle barked.

9

Something plucked at Fargo's sheepskin coat. In a twinkling he drew the Colt and fired at the muzzle flash, and then he was going all out, arms and legs pumping. From the other wagons spilled armed troupe members who hastily crouched and began blasting at the war party. Guns popped like fireworks while above the din rose the whoops of the warriors.

He reached Molly's van, wrenched the door open, and dived inside before a brave could take a bead, rolling on his shoulder as he entered. Sweeping upright, he saw the three women to his right. Abby was on her back, her face pale, her right hand gripping her bloody left shoulder.

Molly was trying to move Abby's hand to examine the wound, but Abby resisted.

At Fargo's entrance, Chelsea turned and said, "She's been nicked in the shoulder. I don't think it's serious."

"You must stay low," Fargo cautioned, moving closer to get them to comply.

The side of the van abruptly splintered inward and Chelsea took a short step, her spine arching, her eyes becoming the size of walnuts. "Oh, my!" she exclaimed, and blood spurted from the corner of her mouth.

Fargo was there in a bound, taking her into his arms. She collapsed limply, confusion lining her countenance as if she couldn't believe she'd been shot.

"Chelsea!" Molly cried, leaping up and dashing over. "No! Not you!"

The Southerner gulped and breathed raggedly, her hands waving feebly in the air. "Molly? What happened to the light?" she asked weakly.

Skye carried her to a bunk and gently set her down. Her raspy breathing told him she'd sustained a severe lung wound, and the crimson frothing her lips told him she wasn't long for this world. He stood back to let Molly lean over her, listening to the gunfire outside, and heard a man scream in anguish.

"What about me?" Abby demanded. "I've been shot too. Or doesn't anyone care?"

He ignored her and ran to the doorway, staying to the left of the jamb to keep from silhouetting himself against the backdrop of the lantern light. A rifle cracked out on the plain and a horse, shot, whinnied pitiably. They were going for the stock!

The insight brought him out of the wagon in a single pantherish leap, the .44 in his right hand as he rushed toward the horses. If the Cheyennes killed them, the troupe would be stranded and have no hope whatsoever of reaching Miller's Crossing. One horse was already down. The rest were milling in panic, some striving to break loose so they could gallop off.

Yet another rifle spat flame out on the snow, then a second, and Fargo answered both with blasts from the Colt. Some of the troupe added their firepower to his, and he detected a fleeing form as it sped off. Once at the string he halted and crouched, the Colt extended, but there were no targets to shoot.

As suddenly as the skirmish began, it ended. All firing by the Cheyennes ceased and they melted away. The company members continued to shoot sporadically for another minute, until Buffalo Briggs bellowed, "Cease firing, you dunderheads! They're gone!"

Fargo went to the Ovaro and verified the stallion was unhurt, then stepped to the downed horse, which kicked spasmodically and neighed faintly. The slug had bored into the animal's broad chest close to the heart, and Fargo knew it would soon expire.

"Did we beat them, boyo?"

Skye shifted. Kevin O'Casey was staring into the distance in abject dread, his rifle clutched in both hands. "We drove them off for a while, but they'll be back."

"I've never been so scared in all my days," Kevin confessed, and trembled. "I loaded and fired as fast as I could and it didn't do a damn bit of good."

"Is there someone on the train skilled at treating wounds besides Molly?"

"There's Jennifer Applegate. Want me to fetch her?"

"Find Frederick and make the rounds of all the wagons. Take Jennifer along. When you're done, let me know where we stand."

"What will you be doing?"

"Making sure the Cheyennes are gone."

"You're going out there?" Kevin said, shocked.

"Someone has to," Fargo said. "Now go find Frederick."

Nodding, O'Casey hastened toward their van. Fargo squatted beside the fallen horse, which was lying as still as a stone and no longer breathing. He double-checked, confirming the animal had died. Then he rose and went to Molly's wagon. She was kneeling next to the bunk bearing Chelsea, her head bowed, crying softly. Fargo didn't need to ask why.

"I liked her," Abby said softly. She was sitting up, her scratch apparently forgotten in the sorrow of the moment. "She reminded me of my mother."

Skye put a hand on Molly's shoulder and she raised tear-filled eyes. "There are others who need you. Frederick and O'Casey are making the rounds. Why don't you lend a hand?" he asked, hoping the activity would lessen her suffering.

"I will," Molly said, sniffling. She stood, clutching his arm for support, and wiped a hand across both cheeks. Her hand brushed Chelsea's arm. "She was the kindest, sweetest soul I ever met. She didn't deserve to die like this."

"No one does," Fargo said, and ushered her to the door. She grabbed her coat, gave his hand an affectionate squeeze, and dashed outside.

"What about me, big man?" Abby inquired, grinning seductively. "Care to bandage me up? While you're at it, you can check my whole body for wounds."

Fargo concealed his disgust by feeding a cartridge into the Sharps. "There's a time and place for everything, Abby," he said, and left. The wagon train was in chaos, with members of the troupe rushing every which way and excitedly comparing notes on the attack. Some tended the wounded. Near the head of the train a man lay sprawled facedown in the cold blanket of snow.

Heading south, Fargo moved bent over to minimize his outline. He cocked the Sharps just in case. Stopping every few feet to crouch and listen, he scoured the pale landscape for the Cheyennes. Not that he expected any to have stuck around. The attack was a harassing ploy, nothing more. Once the Cheyennes believed they had inflicted enough damage, they'd simply vanished. Tomorrow they would strike again, and probably every day after that until the train reached Miller's Crossing or the Cheyennes spilled enough blood to temporarily appease their hatred of all whites.

He suspected this was the same bunch that had struck the other wagon train and that they had ambushed many more. They knew exactly how to sow panic in whites; the night attack, the random firing, and the war whoops were all calculated to cause utter confusion and reap unbridled fear. The strategy had worked marvelously well.

There would have been no evidence the Cheyennes had even been there if not for their tracks, which were too deep to be successfully covered up. They had taken their wounded and dead with them when they faded away like ghosts, as Indians invariably did, and there was no sure means of determining exactly how many had been slain. But Fargo was able to make a reliable guess based on the bloodstains.

After diligent searching, he found the spots where six of the eight warriors had lain. Their impressions were easy to distinguish. So were the dark stains bordering those impressions. From the size of the stains, he concluded that one of the Cheyennes had been wounded and possibly two killed, which was more than he'd dared hope for. There were five, though, who hadn't been touched, and those five were more than enough to wreak havoc with the acting company.

The footprints all led toward the southwest. He figured the Cheyennes had hidden their horses in a convenient stand of trees a fair distance from the wagons. Chasing them would prove pointless since they had either reached their mounts or were almost there. Then, too, he didn't like the idea of chasing them by himself, which he would have to do because there wasn't a single member of the troupe he could rely on not to get himself killed.

He let down the hammer on his rifle and ambled toward the wagons. The worst was yet to come. Depending on how the

Cheyennes went about it, they could make life for the troupe a veritable living hell. And whatever the war party came up with, he must devise a tactic to counter it.

"Halt! Who is that?"

Fargo stopped at the challenge and spied a man near the lead wagon. "It's Skye Fargo," he replied swiftly so the actor wouldn't shoot first and check his identity later. "Don't get trigger-happy on my account."

"Sorry. Come on in."

The camp had quieted down. The initial excitement had been replaced by a sober realization of what had occurred. Three bodies now lay near the second wagon, all on their backs. One of the dead was Chelsea.

Fargo stopped and stared at her features. As with many who died a violent death, her face was oddly composed, serene in the extreme, as if at the instant of dying she had found a source of supreme joy. He'd seen the same look on the faces of countless corpses and wondered how he would look when his time came.

Kevin O'Casey walked up. "I have a final tally for you, boyo," he said despondently. "It's worse than I feared."

"Tell me."

The Irishman nodded at the bodies. "As you can plainly see, we've lost three, and there are six wounded. Most were hit when they rushed outside to see what all the shooting was about. Thankfully, most of the wounds are minor. One man took an arrow in the belly and he's not doing too well. Molly and Jennifer don't know if he'll make it or not."

"It's just the beginning," Fargo said grimly.

"Tom Frederick is in the wagon," O'Casey said. "I've never seen anyone as upset as he is. Blames himself for this whole horrible affair."

"Molly?"

"She's tending to a man who was nicked in the neck."

Around the van on their left walked Buffalo Briggs and Vangent. The wagon boss pointed at the bodies in disgust.

"I've never had this happen on a train I've guided before. Sometimes I think that tenderfeet have no damn business traveling any farther west than Kansas City."

Fargo was sorry Briggs hadn't been one of the casualties. "How many wagon trains have you guided?" he asked innocently.

Buffalo Briggs paused. "Oh, somewhere between twenty and thirty. You lose count after a while." With a curt motion, he led Vangent back the way they had come.

"Do you believe him?" Kevin whispered.

"The man wouldn't know the truth if it shot him," Skye said. There was no way Briggs could have led so many wagon trains westward. If he had, he would have acquired a considerable reputation as a reliable wagon boss and his name would be widely known and highly regarded from the Mississippi River to the Rocky Mountains. And Skye had never heard so much as a mention of the man's name. The evidence kept piling up, proving beyond any doubt that Buffalo Briggs was a fraud. "I'll see you later," he said, and walked toward their wagon.

Up ahead, Abby appeared in the doorway of the van she shared with Molly. In her right hand was a suitcase.

"Going somewhere?" Fargo asked as she climbed down.

She glanced at him in annoyance. "You bet your ass I am. I'm moving in with Leslie and Maggie. I'll be damned if I'll stay with Molly now that I know her true feelings about me." She angrily hefted her bag. "After Chelsea died, I asked her for help and she looked at me as if I was the worst person in the world."

"I thought the two of you were friends."

"Friends? Ha! That's a joke. We've barely tolerated each other. We were always bickering and Chelsea was always there to settle us down. Now she's gone and I don't intend to stay." With that she spun and tramped toward a different van.

Good riddance, Fargo thought, and scanned the camp. Most of the actors and actresses were still outside, talking in hushed tones. Several men had gathered wood and started a large fire near the stock. The troupe members were slowly gravitating toward it. Given what had happened, Fargo doubted many of them would get much sleep.

There was nothing else for him to do. Briggs would arrange a guard schedule and the wounded were being ministered to. He entered his wagon to find Frederick standing next to the stove, his body bowed as if under an enormous weight, his thin hands clasped behind his back.

"Have you ever wanted to curl up in a hole and die?" Frederick asked without facing around.

"At least twice a day."

"I'm serious, Mr. Fargo," Frederick said. "Three fine, innocent people have died and their blood is on my hands. I never should have left Chicago. If I had a shred of intelligence, those three would still be alive."

"Indian attacks are part of the way of life out here," Fargo said. "You can't blame yourself."

"Watch me."

Skye detected a quavering note in Frederick's voice and decided the man would be better off alone. He exited, and with nowhere else to go went to Molly's wagon. To his surprise, she was there, seated on a bunk. "Didn't expect you back so soon," she said.

"Jennifer is handling the last of the wounded. I bumped into Abby and she tore into me, called me every dirty name she knew, and that was a lot," Molly told him, and frowned. "It's been one thing after another tonight. I feel as if I've been wrung out and left to dry."

Skye closed the door, leaned the Sharps in a corner, and removed his coat. "Want me to fix some coffee?"

"You?"

"Why not? A man who spends as much time on the trail as I do has to learn to cook his own grub or become a scarecrow," Fargo replied, and headed for the front of the van.

"No," Molly said, rising to block his path, an unusual glint in her eyes. "I don't need coffee. I want you to hold me."

"What will the rest say if someone walks in on us?" Fargo quipped.

"Frankly, I don't care," Molly said, and stepped close to embrace him, her cheek pressed to his chest. "I need company. I need to know I'm not alone."

"Don't pay attention to what Abby says. You have a lot of friends among the troupe," Fargo consoled her, inhaling the fragrance of her hair. He became conscious of the pressure of her breasts and felt his manhood rouse with interest.

"We're all alone," Molly said quietly.

"I noticed."

"The rest are all busy. No one will bother us."

Skye grinned. "What did you have in mind?"

"This," Molly said, and craned her slender neck to kiss him passionately on the lips. Her arms rose above his shoulders and her fingers looped in his hair.

His hunger fueled by hers, Fargo darted his tongue into her mouth, her sweet saliva mixing with his own to lubricate their mouths as their tongues entwined. He inhaled her hot breath, feeling her hands roam over his broad back, slowly at first but with increasing ardor as her inner fires were kindled and blazed. A soft moan fluttered from deep in her throat and she ground her hips into his.

Skye suddenly realized he'd neglected to lock the door, and since he didn't want anyone to intrude and spoil Molly's mood, he reluctantly broke the kiss. "Hold on a minute," he said huskily.

"What's wrong?"

"Not a thing," Fargo said. She watched him throw the bolt and grinned when he walked back.

"How considerate. I knew that deep down you are a gentleman."

He swept her into his arms again and gave her a kiss she would remember to the end of her days, nearly bending her in half, aroused by the manner in which her legs clung to his. Straightening, he moved her close to the bunk, then gave her a jolt by cupping his right hand to her nether mound at the junction of her thighs.

"Ohhh, Skye!" Molly cried.

Fargo clamped his lips on hers, his left hand swooping to her breasts and alternately massaging both through the material of her dress. Between his tongue and his hands he brought her to a boil. It was like fine-tuning a fiddle or a guitar. The more he caressed her, the more she cooed and ahhhed and squirmed. His manhood was about ready to burst his pants.

"I want you!" Molly said urgently. "Oh, how I want you."

He didn't doubt it for a second. She was an armful, her hands everywhere, her body responsive to his slightest touch. To his delight, she lowered one hand to his groin and stroked his organ, making it iron hard. Placing both hands on her shoulders, he walked her backward to the bunk and eased her onto her back.

Molly grinned, her billowy hair framing her lovely face, and reached up to pull him down. "Do everything to me. I want to experience it all."

"First we get buck naked," Fargo said, and swiftly stripped her, then himself. She was exquisite, her globes like ripe melons waiting to be tasted. Her silken legs quivered uncontrollably. And her slit, when he inched a finger between her thighs, was moist with desire. He traced a path from her chin to her navel, kissing and licking in a beeline to her sexual core. Then, when she had no idea what to expect and was braced for anything, he dropped his mouth to her love tunnel and tasted her essence.

"Oh, my!" Molly cried, and bucked her hips wildly. "I feel . . . I feel . . ."

Whatever she felt, she didn't say. Fargo gave her tunnel the same treatment he'd given her mouth and breasts, and she responded by locking her legs around his head as if trying to envelop him in her body. For another five minutes he steadily heightened her ecstasy. Not until she thrashed and moaned and wrenched on his hair did he rise on his knees, grip his organ, and bury himself to the hilt in her wet slit.

Immediately Molly was overcome by unrestrained carnal lust. She became as much a wildcat as Abby—even more so. She kissed and rubbed and heaved in blissful abandon. "Ooooooh, yes! Oh, please, please, please!"

Fargo knew what she wanted, and he gave it to her, pounding into her tunnel like a stallion into a mare, the two of them rocking the bunk so hard it shook underneath them. He tried to hold out, to last indefinitely, but Molly began wiggling in a way that drove him crazy with desire.

"Skye!" she squealed. "I'm coming! I'm coming!"

And so was he, driving into her as if there would be no tomorrow, spurting faster than a fire hose, spurting on and on and on until they clasped one another tightly and held firm, their bodies joined as one. They coasted to an eventual stop, each totally spent, each, for the moment, satisfied and at peace. But in the back of Fargo's mind he was already thinking about dawn and the return of the war party.

10

By noon the next day the Cheyennes had still not put in an appearance.

Fargo didn't know what to make of it. He'd been up well before dawn to feed and saddle the Ovaro, then he'd helped get the teams ready. All the while he kept scouring the countryside for the war party, but the only living thing he saw was a solitary raven winging from west to east. Once the wagons were underway, he breathed a little easier. But not much.

The mood of the Frederick Repertory Troupe could only be described as somber. Few spoke. Most took a few moments before departing that morning to stand by the three fresh graves at the side of the trail and offer their silent last respects to their unfortunate companions.

Buffalo Briggs rode at the head of the column. Kevin O'Casey and two other men, astride several of their spare horses, rode with him. Vangent drove Molly's wagon.

Staring at her wagon now with the sun almost directly overhead, Fargo recollected their lovemaking and grinned contentedly. Once her passion had been unchained, she'd turned into an insatiable vixen. She'd made love to him until the wee hours of the morning and might have continued until daylight if he hadn't needed to catch some sleep. Quite a woman, that Molly Howard. One day she'd meet some lucky gent who would have the good sense to marry her and probably wind up dying in bed.

Skye stayed on the move, patroling around the wagons again and again, riding far enough out to be able to give advance warning should the Cheyennes appear. They would, eventually. It was a matter of timing. At the time and place of their choosing they would spring an ambush. He had to outguess them and figure out where the ambush would take place, and outguessing Indians wasn't easy.

The wagon train was on a straight stretch where there were

few drifts, making fast headway. To the right a break in the ice showed the sluggishly flowing water of the Solomon River. There was brush along the bank and a few trees to the south. Buffalo Briggs raised his right hand, signalling their midday halt, and the drivers gratefully hauled on the ribbons.

Fargo conducted another sweep for good measure before turning and riding to Molly's van. The door was open and from inside came soft, contented humming and the sound of a pan rattling on the griddle. He tied the reins to the rear wheel and went in.

Molly heard him and turned, her radiant smile warming the interior more than the potbellied stove. "Since you didn't bother to eat breakfast, I thought I'd make some flapjacks for you. Hope you're hungry."

"Yep. Surprising, too."

"How so?"

"After all the eating I did last night, you'd figure I wouldn't need to eat again for a week."

Her brow furrowed; then she caught the double meaning and laughed lustily, her face becoming a vivid shade of crimson as she did. "Skye, please! What if someone heard you?"

"Last night you didn't care one way or the other," Fargo said, walking forward.

Molly glanced at the door. "Last night I wasn't thinking straight. All I wanted was you."

Skye grinned. "You didn't hear me complain." He gave her a peck on the cheek.

"Now don't start. The wagons will be moving out again in half an hour," Molly said, then suddenly looked at her pan in alarm. "Drat! I'm burning the flapjacks." She grabbed the flapjack turner and flipped over the two large flapjacks with deft efficiency.

Fargo took a seat on a bunk and unbuttoned his coat. His eyes hurt from having spent so many hours contending with the harsh glare of the snow, and he rubbed them to alleviate the discomfort.

"We don't have much flour left," Molly commented.

"I know. Everyone is low," Fargo said. "I've been looking for animal sign all morning but haven't found anything. If we're lucky we'll come across some deer before too long."

"And if we're not lucky?"

"There are enough spare horses to tide us over for a few days."

"Eat the horses? Oh, how disgusting. I could never do such a thing."

"If you get hungry enough, you'll eat anything," Fargo said. "It won't kill you to eat a horse. Some Indians do it all the time. The Apaches, in particular, although they like mule meat better."

"Are you kidding me?"

"Nope. The Apaches consider mule meat the tastiest there is. They'll gorge themselves on it until they're ready to bust a seam."

"You certainly do know a lot about Indians," Molly said. She put the flapjacks on a plate and brought it over along with a knife and fork.

"Aren't you eating?" Skye asked.

"I munched on a cookie this morning," Molly said. She handed the plate to him, then stepped to a cabinet. "I have some sugar left here somewhere."

"Don't bother," Fargo said, and greedily tore into the flapjacks with his fork. They were delicious, and he told her as much.

"I could cook by the time I was eight," Molly said proudly. "My mother—God rest her soul—was from the old school that believed a girl should know how to cook, sew, and clean before she was ten."

"A man could pack on the pounds living with you," Fargo said, and saw her features cloud. Was she thinking of her husband? He quickly changed the subject. "I'll be riding farther out this afternoon to find game. If I don't show up by dark, don't let that fool Briggs send out anyone after me."

"Do you think he would?"

"The old Briggs, no. But this new, friendly version has me stumped. I can't figure out what he's up to," Fargo said, chewing heartily. He swallowed, then gazed at the bullet hole in the side of the van. She had stuffed part of a rag into it to keep out the cold. "If the Cheyennes attack while I'm gone, lock the door and stay low. Lie on the floor. I don't want them to get you like they did Chelsea."

"Thank you," she said softly.

"Can you use a gun?"

"I've never shot one in my life."

Easterners, Fargo reflected in annoyance. Many of them had no business braving the Plains and the Rockies when they didn't even have the knowhow to defend themselves from a feisty raccoon. "If I ever get the time, I'll teach you," he offered, and continued eating. She sat silently watching him until the last morsel was swallowed and he licked his lips in satisfaction.

"I've never met a man who lives life so fully," Molly remarked thoughtfully.

"What?" Fargo said, puzzled by what she meant.

"Everything you do, you do with zest," Molly said. "You eat as if each meal is your last, you make love as if there will be no tomorrow, and you live every moment with relish. You're not like most men I know. They coast through life without ever living it." She paused and scowled. "I know, because I've lived the same way. I think it's time I learned to live all over again, to get the most out of life like you do."

"I never gave the matter much thought," Fargo said, although inwardly he agreed with her in at least one respect. He *did* like to get the most out of love-making. Bedding a pretty woman was one of the supreme enjoyments in life.

They made small talk until they heard Buffalo Briggs bellowing for everyone to get ready to move out. Fargo thanked her for the grub, kissed her, and went out into the bright sunlight to mount the Ovaro. Heading west to scout the countryside, he passed Briggs.

"Strange we haven't seen hide nor hair of those Injuns yet," the wagon boss commented.

"They'll pick their own time and place," Skye said.

"Where's an army patrol when you need one?"

Fargo kept riding, sticking to the Solomon River Trail. He wondered idly if those shod tracks he'd seen when he first located the trail after the blizzard had been made by a patrol, then discounted the idea because there had only been four riders in the group and a patrol would have included eight men or more. The blowing wind and drifting snow had long since obliterated those tracks, and he knew the quartet was somewhere ahead of the wagon train and likewise making for Miller's Crossing.

Hours elapsed uneventfully. He rode well in front of the vans, alone in the shimmering sea of white, squinting to reduce the risk of snow blindness. The temperature climbed well into the forties or low fifties and the snow was melting rapidly. If the warm spell persisted, all of the snow would be gone in another two to three days.

Toward sunset he drew rein beside a point where the ice had all gone from the river and the water flowed sluggishly. To the south lay a small tract of trees. The site was ideal for making camp and he rode in a circle checking for the Cheyennes before returning to the middle of the trail and waiting for the wagons to catch up.

In due course the column appeared, Briggs, O'Casey, and three other men riding in advance. Kevin waved and Skye reciprocated, and his arm was still in the air when the crack of a rifle shot rolled across the Plains. He saw one of the men clutch at his chest and topple from the saddle, and he spurred the Ovaro into a gallop while palming the Colt.

The wagon train was over a hundred yards off. Briggs and the men were unlimbering their hardware and scouring the snow for the source of the shot. The wagon drivers had prudently stopped, each man grabbing a rifle from the seat beside him.

"Take cover!" Fargo shouted, knowing the riders and drivers were easy targets astride their mounts or perched in the wagon seats. They were greenhorns who didn't know enough to get down when being ambushed, and they'd pay the price if they didn't start moving fast.

Another rifle shot cracked. The driver of the first van went off his seat as if he'd been kicked by a Missouri mule, his rifle flying from his fingers.

Fargo rode at a gallop, keeping low, somewhat surprised there seemed to be only one attacker. He guessed the warrior doing the firing was to the south of the train, but he couldn't see anyone. The brave was well hidden. But then he spotted a puff of gun smoke hovering over a drift sixty yards off and cut the stallion toward it.

The rifle banged again, only this time the warrior had shifted position.

Fargo heard an angry buzz, as if a bee had just flown past, and he sent two rounds into the drift, spacing the shots a foot or so apart. Suddenly the drift erupted upward with snow spraying in all directions and a stocky Cheyenne heaved to his feet and cradled a rifle to his shoulder. Fargo never hesitated. He employed an old Comanche trick, swinging down on the side of the stallion to expose as little of himself as possible. The warrior fired once more without effect.

Keeping his left arm and leg hooked over the Ovaro, Fargo extended his right arm and tried to get a bead on the brave. The bobbing gait made pinpoint accuracy impossible, and the best he could do was aim at the warrior's chest and fire, hoping to score.

The Cheyenne stumbled backward, then steadied himself and again tucked his rifle to his shoulder.

In a flash of insight Fargo realized what the warrior might do, what he himself would do if the situation were reversed and he was being charged by an Indian riding in a similiar fashion. Instead of trying to nail the rider, which would be extremely difficult, he'd go for the easy shot and down the horse to prevent the rider from getting any closer. Killing a horse was a last resort, but better a horse should die than himself.

The moment the insight struck, he pushed off from the Ovaro and dropped. He didn't want the stallion killed, whatever the cost. The Ovaro was the best and most intelligent horse he'd ever owned, and he rated it as worth its weight in solid gold. In a land where a man's life might well depend on the speed, stamina, and alertness of his mount, a good horse was invaluable.

So Skye let go and dropped, counting on the snow to cushion his fall and prevent a broken bone. His right shoulder hit and he rolled, surging to one knee as the warrior fired and missed. He took deliberate aim, compensating for the yardage by elevating the barrel a hair. At his shot the Cheyenne spun and then sprawled forward, arms outflung.

Silence prevailed. Fargo heard the whisper of the breeze and the sound of horses approaching from the trail. The Ovaro had gone a dozen yards and halted and was now looking back at him expectantly. He slowly stood, the Colt cocked in case the warrior was playing possum. Advancing carefully, he nudged the body with a toe. The warrior was dead.

"Were you hit, boyo?" O'Casey asked.

"No."

"Looks like he was," Briggs said. "He's got three holes in him."

Fargo nodded, staring at the blood-rimmed exit holes in the brave's neck. He began extracting the spent cartridges from the Colt and replacing them with shells from his gunbelt.

"Where are the rest of them?" Kevin inquired. "Why was there just this one?"

"There are too many of us for them to risk an all-out attack," Fargo answered, "so they're trying to whittle us down bit by bit. They'll have a few more nasty surprises in store for us before they're done." He glanced at the shattered drift and saw the excavated space where the brave had hidden after burrowing into the drift from the rear. Behind the drift were moccasin tracks, three sets in all. Three warriors had ridden to the spot and one had remained to spring the ambush while the others had taken their mounts off to the southwest. The man who had remained must have known he would probably be caught and killed, yet he'd dug out the hole and prepared a firing slit in the snow anyway.

Indians seldom sacrificed themselves needlessly. Fargo remembered the wind had been stronger earlier, and he speculated that the Cheyenne had counted on the gun smoke being dispersed before his hiding place could be discovered. The Colt reloaded, Skye slid the gun into his holster and retrieved the Ovaro.

O'Casey shadowed him. "Is there anything we can do to prevent something like that from happening again?"

"Not much. We can post outriders on all sides. The war party will still find a way at us, even if they only pick off the outriders," Fargo said, climbing into the saddle.

"Lord, I hate this. I feel so damned helpless. Those red devils can pick us off at their leisure, as if we're targets in a shooting gallery."

"We are," Fargo said, goading the stallion toward the vans. Most of the troupe now stood outside, many gathered around the fallen men.

Molly was walking away from the downed driver, her shoulders slumped.

"Dead?" Skye asked, stopping.

She nodded. "At this rate there won't be enough of us left to do a soliloquy by the time we reach Denver."

"Most of us will make it," Fargo predicted.

"But not all. And I can't help but worry that I might not be one of the lucky ones."

Fargo dismounted and lent a hand bedding the horses down for the night. He selected a spot near the trees where the animals would be partially sheltered from the cold night wind, then helped pick three men who would stand the first watch. Buffalo Briggs stayed close to him, and once again the wagon boss was a model of politeness. Fargo continued to suspect the man had an ulterior motive but had no idea what it might be.

While the stock was being tended, the two men who had been slain were buried near the river. Every actor and actress in the company turned out to hear a few proper words offered by Tom Frederick.

Once, as Fargo worked at tying one of the horses, he glanced at the assembled troupe and spotted Abby staring at him. As soon as he noticed, she abruptly stopped. He continued working, and when he was done went to Molly's van for his evening meal.

"I'm sorry," she apologized as she stood at the stove. "I can scrape together some weak soup and that's it. The cupboard is almost empty."

"I'll try again tomorrow to bag game."

Molly looked at him and mustered a feeble grin. The burials had shaken her, leaving her preoccupied and much quieter than usual. "If you see any mules, shoot one. Any meat would be good right about now."

Skye ate with relish, and he was almost done when there came a knock at the door and Tom Frederick peeked inside.

"Mind if I intrude?"

"Of course not," Molly responded. "Come on in."

Frederick entered and sat on a bunk across from Fargo.

"Sorry to bother you, but I had an idea and I wanted to ask your opinion."

"I'm listening," Fargo said. The man had a haggard appearance, the result of the sustained strain they were all under. Or perhaps it was worse for Frederick since he was the head of the troupe and felt responsible for the lives of everyone in his employ.

"As I'm sure you're aware, we're critically short on provisions," Frederick began. "We're proceeding much slower than I'd anticipated and soon we'll be completely out of food."

"There's not much we can do except tighten our belts and hope I find a deer or two."

"I've been thinking about the problem. What if you were to ride on to Miller's Crossing and bring back enough supplies to see us safely there?"

"It would take days."

"But at least we'd be assured of food eventually."

"And in the meantime? You folks aren't accustomed to going without three squares a day. You'd have to turn to eating your stock, and with fewer horses you'd have to leave some of the vans behind." Fargo shook his head. "No, I figure it's smarter for me to stay with the wagon train."

Frederick opened his mouth to object.

"Besides," Fargo went on quickly, "how many of you are skilled hunters? How many of you could put meat on the table? How many of you could ride off across the snow and find your way back without becoming lost?"

"None of us," Frederick admitted rather reluctantly.

"Then I'm not going anywhere." Fargo rose and handed his bowl to Molly. "Tomorrow I'll look far and wide for game. Even though buffalo aren't in this area now, there are still scattered groups of deer. I won't come back until I get one."

"Thank you," Frederick said, and glanced at the doorway. He lowered his voice when next he spoke. "There is something else I'd like to discuss. I've come to rely on your judgment much more than Buffalo Briggs's, and the latest incidents have me stumped."

"What incidents?"

"Someone has been searching the vans. Two troupe members

have reported returning to their wagons to find drawers and closets open and belongings scattered about. The vans are always unoccupied when it occurs.''

"Has anything been stolen?"

"Evidently not, which only adds to the mystery," Frederick said. "The first incident occurred the other day when everyone was outside after the Indian attack. The second took place earlier when everyone attended the burials." He paused. "Someone must have slipped away unnoticed and gone through the vans."

"Why?" Molly threw in. "What are they looking for?"

"I wish I knew," Tom Frederick said. "It makes no sense that I can see."

Fargo poured himself a cup of steaming coffee from the pot Molly had made, then sat down. There might be a connection between the searches and the deaths of Schweer and Wehner. Since no personal effects had been stolen, it clearly meant someone was after something specific. What, he didn't know. But perhaps it was valuable. He well knew how greedy men could be and how some would stop at nothing, not even murder, to gain wealth.

"Do you have any ideas?" Frederick asked.

"Not yet," Fargo said. "But maybe you'd better have someone you trust keep an eye on the vans from here on out. Maybe we'll catch whoever it is in the act."

"I could ask Kevin O'Casey to watch the wagons. He's as reliable as they come."

Fargo liked the choice and said so.

"Good. I'll go talk to him," Frederick said, rising. "Then I think I'll turn in early. I haven't been sleeping well."

From outside, at the rear of the van, came a slight thump as if someone had rapped on the wood. Fargo was on his feet and out the door in a rush. He jumped to the ground and rushed to the back of the wagon but found no one there. Twilight had descended, and in the dim light boot prints were visible beside the van. Someone had been eavesdropping, heard Frederick say he was leaving, and turned to run off but slipped in the slick snow. Fargo glanced the length of the wagon train and was just in time to see someone dart around the second wagon down. It was a brief glimpse, but enough for him to identify the man.

Vangent.

11

Fargo took a stride after the teamster, then stopped. It wouldn't do any good to confront Vangent and accuse him of eavesdropping. It would be Vangent's word against his, and Vangent could always claim he'd just been out walking. Besides, the vans were well constructed and the sides were thick. He doubted Vangent could have heard much. Then he saw the glimmer of light.

On the left side, within inches of the corner, a thin ray of light emanated from within. He leaned forward and discovered a thin crack. From the chipped condition of its edges, he gathered that someone had used a knife to dig into the wood for the specific purpose of being able to hear whatever transpired inside. He pressed an ear to the slit and heard Molly's voice.

" . . . was that all about? Should we go after him?"

"No. We'll stay put until he gets back. There might be trouble."

Skye straightened and frowned. How long had that crack been there? It must have been made when the wagon was empty, and could have been done at any time since the troupe started on its journey. Acting on a hunch, he went to the rear of the next wagon and inspected the wood. Shifting from right to left to study the panel at different angles, he found another slit near the bottom.

A gust of cold wind struck his face and he walked toward Molly's van. He figured if he checked every van, he'd find the same thing. Someone had been spying on the troupe from the beginning. But who was behind it? He knew it couldn't be Vangent; the teamster was barely bright enough to come in out of the rain. And Buffalo Briggs, the next logical suspect, didn't impress him as being overly intelligent either. So there must be someone else. Who, and what were they after?

Molly was standing in the doorway, her shawl around her

shoulders, when he appeared. "What happened? Why did you run out like that?"

Fargo climbed in, closed the door, and motioned for Frederick to move closer. Speaking in a whisper, he divulged what he'd found.

"How dare they!" Tom Frederick blurted. "I'll fire Vangent this minute."

"No," Fargo said.

"No?"

"We know Vangent and Briggs are up to no good. But they don't know that we know. We should go on as if nothing is wrong and keep our eyes on them. Sooner or later we might learn what is behind all of this."

"All right," Frederick said reluctantly. "Can I tell Kevin O'Casey?"

"Him, but no one else."

When they were alone, Molly stepped up to Skye and put her hands on his broad shoulders. "What does it all mean? Where is all of this leading?"

"I don't know," Fargo admitted. "But before this is done, there will be hell to pay."

He was up before daylight and fixed himself a pot of coffee, a weak pot because there wasn't much coffee left. Frederick, Pete, and O'Casey were alseep in their bunks, with Kevin snoring loud enough to rouse the dead. Although Molly had wanted him to spend the night with her, he'd declined. He'd known the busy day that lay ahead of him and he'd wanted to be refreshed for the long hours of riding he had to do. A night of intense love-making would have left him greatly fatigued, and with a war party in the area he wanted to be at his fighting best.

After drinking a steaming cup of the black brew, he donned his coat and went outside. To the east a reddish glow heralded the arrival of the new day. He saddled the Ovaro, took an extra horse to use as his pack animal, and headed to the south, checking for sign every foot of the way.

He must find game today. No matter what, the company must have food. He rode in an arc from west to east, then swung westward again. Twice he saw rabbit prints but they were old and the drifting snow had partially covered them.

At last an oasis of vegetation materialized to the southwest. He rode toward it warily, the Sharps cradled in the crook of his left elbow. The stand turned out to be about thirty yards in diameter. He rode around it, checking for sign, and saw no evidence that unshod horses had been there. He did find deer tracks leading from the trees, going almost due south. Dismounting, he examined the tracks closely and decided they had been made the evening before. Five deer, a buck and four does. Tying the horses to a limb, he opened his saddlebags and took out the roll of heavy twine Molly had given him the previous night. Then he entered the stand and searched the brush until he came upon a rabbit run.

Kneeling at a spot where low bushes flanked the run, he drew his toothpick and cut some twine from the roll. It took but a minute to set up the snare the way he wanted. He walked on, found an interesting run, and set up a second snare there.

Wheeling, he returned to the Ovaro, got into the saddle, and headed south. He replaced the twine while scanning the landscape. Somewhere out there were those deer, and he wasn't going back to the wagon train until he'd bagged meat for the table.

He rode hard. The snow level had dropped considerably, and the unseasonable warmth of the day helped to melt the snow even more. The stallion moved effortlessly, eating up the miles.

Deer, like most animals, were creatures of habit. They stuck to a regular routine most of the time. At night they moved, foraging and going to water. During the day they tended to hole up in the heaviest undergrowth they could find, perhaps grazing a bit but not moving around too much in order to avoid being spotted by predators.

Fargo counted on that fact to enable him to overtake the group. He stayed alongside their trail, and within six miles came to another, larger, stand. Instead of riding in and possibly spooking them if they were there, he rode around the perimeter and found where they had emerged on the southeast side and traveled in that direction.

The sun hung at the midday mark when he spied another island of trees up ahead, the largest so far, and he slowed, the Sharps snug in his left arm. Again he went around the stand, only this time he found no evidence the deer had left. They were still in there.

He drew rein on the south side, tied the horses, and bent at the waist before stealthily slipping into the brush. If he was right, the deer would be bedded down near the center of the stand. With their keen hearing and smell they undoubtedly knew he was there, but they wouldn't know exactly where if he could move quietly enough as he closed in on them.

A lifetime of living in the rugged wilderness had honed his hunting ability until he could move like an Indian when need be. He placed each foot down with the utmost care, avoiding twigs or branches that might break and give him away. His feet made no noise.

The wind was blowing from the northwest to the southeast, so even though the deer had picked up his scent when he first neared the stand, they now couldn't pinpoint him by his smell. He avoided projecting branches that would brush his clothing and froze every second or third step to listen and look.

Once the deer knew he was stalking them, they'd be off like a shot. He must be ready to fire on an instant because he might only get one chance. His gaze strayed to the Sharps and he frowned. He'd neglected to cock the rifle before entering the stand, and if he did so now they might hear the click. But it couldn't be helped. As gently as possible to reduce the noise, he thumbed the hammer back, then continued.

Ten yards farther he suddenly halted. Something had moved off to his left, and he stayed immobile as he studied the trees and the bushes, seeking the cause. Abruptly he saw them, all five deer. They were strung out in a line, the buck in the lead, and making for the west side of the stand using every available cover. The buck paused now and again to sniff the air and look about, but it was clear they hadn't spotted Fargo yet.

He pressed the stock to his shoulder. Immediately the big buck saw him and took a leap, heading for thicker undergrowth. Fargo sighted and fired in the same breath and saw the buck go down. Fingers flying, he worked the lever, lowering the breechlock to gain access to the chamber. It took all of two seconds to insert a new cartridge and lift the gun, but by then the four does were in full flight and scattering in different directions.

He took a bead on a large doe racing to the northwest. In three bounds she would be in deep cover. He took her on the second, the Sharps booming and bucking and the shot catching her at the base of her neck as she coiled her legs for another bound. Down she went, sliding several feet before she crashed into a tree and lay still.

Fargo rose and sprinted forward. Deer were hardy animals and a single shot, no matter how well placed, often failed to kill one. Wounded deer had been known to travel miles leaking blood by the gallon, and he had no desire to chase one halfway to the Rockies.

The buck was on its knees and struggling to rise, snorting and grunting. It turned to face him, and with deliberate aim he shot it between the eyes. Turning, he ran to the doe. It was dead.

Skye replaced the spent round in his six-shooter, holstered the gun, and went to the horses. Taking a rope, he walked to the buck, which was bleeding profusely. He didn't want to get blood all over his buckskins so he tied loops around its front legs and hauled it out of the stand. With the war party still abroad he couldn't afford to be gone from the wagon train for longer than absolutely necessary. He intended to butcher both animals once he caught up with the train.

Dragging both deer out and lifting them onto the pack horse required the better part of half an hour. He lifted carefully to avoid getting blood on himself. Once the deer were draped over the horse, he tied them down securely, mounted the Ovaro, and retraced his route toward the Solomon River Trail.

It was late afternoon when he came to the stand where he'd set the snares, and he took the time to check them. One was empty, but the other contained a large rabbit already dead. He removed both snares, then added the rabbit to his spoils. When back in the saddle, he pushed the horses to reach the trail before dark.

The sun had set and the sky was filled with stars when he finally reached the ruts in the snow that marked the passage of the vans. He turned westward and headed after them, knowing it would be pushing midnight before he caught up with the wagons.

All around him was still except for the gurgling of the river where the ice had melted. The wind had temporarily died. The ride gave him time to think, to ponder the sequence of events since he'd hooked up with the acting troupe and to try and make sense of the whole affair. He reviewed all he knew but could reach no conclusions other than the obvious.

Someone—or maybe it was more than one person—wanted something that might be hidden in one of the vans.

These parties were willing to kill to get it.

Briggs and Vangent were probably working for someone else, but he had no idea who.

In the end, he thought in circles and was no closer to solving the mystery. He took a breath and thought about Molly instead, and of her passionate love-making. Another night with her was in order.

From far off to the west came the faint crack of a shot.

Fargo spurred the Ovaro into a gallop. As he did, he heard other shots, a flurry of gunfire as if a full-scale battle was in progress. It could only mean one thing. The wagon train was under attack.

He could make faster time if he left the pack horse behind, but those people needed food desperately. So he clung to the lead rope and galloped into the night, covering almost a mile before he reached a low rise in the road. He slowed, hearing loud retorts from the other side. Advancing cautiously, he halted shy of the crest and slid down, whipping the Sharps out as his feet touched the ground.

Hunkered down, he crept to the top and peered over. Sixty yards away, in a narrow hollow through which the trail meandered, were the wagons. Men were shooting and yelling back and forth. There were no campfires and he could distinguish few details, but he thought he saw a number of harness horses down.

The men were shooting at the low ridge on the south side of the trail. A flash of flame blossomed as someone on the ridge returned the fire.

It had to be the Cheyennes.

Fargo slipped back to the horses and led them to the side of the trail, where he tied them to a lone bush. Hurrying southward, he swung in a wide loop, planning to come up on the ridge from the rear and take the Indians by surprise. He had to hand it to those braves. They'd hit the wagon train at one of the few spots along the trail where the terrain worked in their favor. From the hollow to Miller's Crossing the ground was flat and open all the way.

He figured the warriors would be concentrating on the vans. They'd have no reason to be gazing out over the plain, and he should be able to get so close they'd never know what hit them. How many would there be? That was the crucial question. Even with the element of surprise on his side, he'd be hard-pressed to slay three or four. Any more than that and he was in big trouble.

He expected there had been casualties among the acting company and he hoped Molly wasn't among them. If the Cheyennes had taken to punching shots into the vans, there might be many hurt or dying. He must turn the tables quickly.

When about fifty yards from the trail, he swung westward and angled in toward the ridge. He went slowly, staying low. As much as he wanted to aid those pilgrims, he wouldn't do them any good if he became careless and was killed. So he took it a step at a time, and after going fifteen yards he heard the whinny of a horse.

To his left were four horses waiting for their riders. They were staring at him, their ears pricked.

Had the Cheyennes heard the whinny? He kept going, every sense alert, concentrating on the dark outline of the ridge. Five more yards he covered. Then ten. He stopped, seeking a telltale silhouette at which he could fire, when the soft pad of rushing feet brought him around to the right just in time to deflect the downward swipe of a tomahawk with his Sharps.

The warrior slammed into him and they both went down, the Indian hissing like a snake. Skye drove the rifle stock into the side of the man's head and the Cheyenne fell to one side, then scrambled upright with the swiftness of a cat.

On one knee, Skye ducked under a vicious swing, then rammed the heavy barrel into the warrior's midsection, doubling the brave over. He rose, sweeping the barrel down and in and striking the warrior full on the face. The man's nose crunched and he flipped onto his back, an inky stain spreading over his features.

The Cheyenne struggled feebly to rise.

Anxious to end the fight before other warriors appeared, Fargo took a step and rammed the rifle stock into the brave's forehead. The heavy wood hit hard and the brave slumped, out cold, blood seeping from his split skin.

Spinning, Skye crouched and leveled the Sharps, ready to cut loose. But there was no one coming at him. The other warriors, wherever they were, were too preoccupied to have noticed the whinny or the fight. He scooted toward the rim and saw a muzzle flash when one of the Cheyennes fired down at the wagon train. Slowing, he narrowed the gap and was at last able to make out the back of a brave in the act of reloading a rifle.

Fargo could have squeezed the trigger and been done with it. To shoot a man in the back, though, even a renegade Indian who deserved to be planted six feet under, went against his grain. His finger tightened but he hesitated, then whispered, "Hey."

The brave whirled, his mouth widening in amazement even as the Sharps thundered. The impact sent the Cheyenne back over the rim and down the snow-covered slope beyond.

From Fargo's right came a surprised exclamation in the Cheyenne tongue, and then he saw a lean figure sprinting toward him. The brave held a bow. With the Sharps in his left hand, Fargo drew with his right, the Colt flashing out and stabbing lead and smoke at the onrushing warrior.

The man buckled, then sprawled motionless on the white mantle.

A roar of rage erupted to Skye's rear and iron arms encircled him from behind. He was lifted bodily and shaken violently from side to side as if he weighed no more than an empty potato sack. The Sharps flew from his fingers and he nearly lost his grip on the Colt. Of a sudden he was flung into the snow, facedown, and when he attempted to push upright a heavy body pounced on his back, flattening him. Hands of stone clamped on his chin and a knee gouged into his spine.

Fargo winced when his head was pulled sharply upward, his neck bent at an unnatural angle. He knew what his adversary was trying to do and had to stop it in the next few seconds or suffer a snapped spinal cord. Pain flooded through him. Gritting his teeth, he tried to throw the brave off, but the man clung to him with the tenacity of a snapping turtle. And each second brought his head farther back. Each moment of delay brought death that much nearer.

He bunched his broad shoulders and tried to throw the warrior over his head. It was like trying to move an anvil. Thwarted, the pain increasing terribly, he twisted his gun hand, wildly slanting the barrel back and up. He wasn't sure he'd hit a thing, but the shots might cause the brave to let go and they were the only chance he had.

So he fired, just once, his consciousness swirling as he squeezed the trigger, and the brave dived to the left to avoid other shots. Dazed, Fargo shoved to his knees and attempted to bring the six-shooter to bear. A moccasin-covered foot swept out of the dark, striking his wrist with the force of a hammer, and the Colt flew into the snow.

Shaking his head to clear his thoughts, Fargo managed to stand. And there, leering at him a yard away, was the muscular warrior who led the war party. The Cheyenne whipped out a knife, grinned, and lunged.

12

Frantically, Fargo threw himself backward and slipped in the treacherous snow. His feet arced out from under him. He landed on his back, his head striking the rim. Looming above him, still grinning, certain of an easy kill, was the Cheyenne.

Perhaps because the firing from the ridge had ceased, so had the shooting from the wagons. The night was strangely quiet, so quiet both men could hear the other breathe.

The warrior raised the knife for another swipe.

In a burst of motion, Skye slammed his boot heel into the brave's leg and rolled to the left. The Cheyenne swung, but the kick had thrown him slightly off balance and the keen blade sank into the snow instead of into Skye.

On his left side, Fargo flicked his right leg up, hitting the muscular warrior in the cheek. The brave glided to one side, out of range of those heavy boots. Which was exactly what Fargo wanted. In a smooth forward roll he rose into a crouch, and as he did his right hand gripped the hilt of the Arkansas toothpick and pulled it free. He held the knife close to his leg, not wanting the Cheyenne to know he had it.

The warrior was a skilled knife fighter. He crouched and swung the knife from right to left, giving no indication of the angle he would use to attack. The grin never left his face, a grin of triumph although he had yet to score so much as a nick.

Fargo held himself low, the knife tucked against his pants. He bobbed and weaved his torso to counter the swings of the brave's knife. To his surprise, the brave abruptly stopped.

"I know you, Trailsman," the man stated harshly. "I see you once at Fort Laramie."

Now that Fargo had a moment to stare at his enemy's face closely, there was something vaguely familiar about the Cheyenne. But he couldn't quite place him.

"Do you remember me?"

"No."

"You forget Fetches-the-Woman?" the brave said skeptically, and edged his right foot a bit closer.

The named jarred Fargo's memory. It had been over two years ago. He'd only been passing through the region and had stopped at Fort Laramie to buy a few provisions. There had been a white woman taken captive from a wagon train and raped and killed by a young Cheyenne warrior who had counted coup on her husband and brother. The troopers had brought in the warrior their informers claimed was responsible, but the survivors of the attack were unable to make a positive identification. So the brave went free. Later, Fargo had heard tell the troopers had the right man all along and he had adopted the new name of Fetches-the-Woman. So this was the same bastard.

"I not forget you," Fetches-the-Woman said, and edged his left foot closer. "A white man point at you when you come out of trading post and tell me who you are. He say you kill many Indians, and laugh. I think then that one day I hope to kill you."

Frago neither responded nor moved. He braced himself for the warrior's next move.

"I see you with these whites and I remember you," the Cheyenne said, and suddenly his voice rose in a raging bellow. "And now I kill!"

But Fargo was ready. The tip of the brave's knife speared at his chest. With a deft shift of both feet and by twisting his body sideways, he avoided the knife. Then, in the same motion, his right arm stabbed the toothpick up and into Fetches-the-Woman's chest.

The Cheyenne gasped and took a step backward.

Or tried to, because Fargo had no intention of showing any mercy. He also took a step, the Arkansas toothpick embedded to the hilt, and cut downward, slicing through the yielding flesh as easily as a saber through a melon, until the blade contacted bone. Wrenching the toothpick out, he moved to one side in case Fetches-the-Woman tried to come at him again.

Gasping louder, the warrior let go of his knife and pressed both hands to his chest. He staggered, his fingers becoming coated with blood, and sank to his knees. Throwing back his head, he began to sing his death chant. He managed only a little, and then he shuddered, wheezed, ceased breathing, and pitched onto his face.

"That's for the woman you raped and killed," Fargo muttered, and bent over to wipe the toothpick clean on the Cheyenne's leggings. Replacing the knife in his boot, he immediately searched the snow for his guns. The Sharps, being long and large, was easily found, but it took all of ten minutes to find where the pistol had vanished under the snow. He wiped it off as best he could on his sleeve, then inserted fresh cartridges.

No other Indians showed up.

Three were definitely dead, but he thought the brave he'd slugged with the Sharps might still be alive. He walked to where the man had fallen, but the Cheyenne was gone. Hurrying to the war horses, he found one missing. The brave, severely wounded, had departed in haste, perhaps after seeing Fetches-the-Woman go down, but in his haste the wounded man had neglected to take the other horses.

Fargo grabbed hold of their rope reins and led them to the spot where the Ovaro and the pack horse waited. Mounting stiffly, his muscles aching from the fight, he rode along the trail until he was near enough to the wagons to be heard clearly. "Don't shoot!" he shouted, concerned as ever that one of the nervous troupe might fire at him first and see who it was later. "It's me, Fargo!"

Shouts broke out all along the line of wagons.

"Get under cover, boyo!" Kevin O'Casey warned. "There's Injuns up on that there rise."

"Not anymore," Fargo replied, coming to the last wagon. A body lay a few feet from the rear wheel, an actor he'd seen about the camp on occasion.

O'Casey hurried up, a rifle clutched in his hand. "We heard shooting up there. Would that have been you?"

"I took care of them," Fargo said.

"All by your lonesome? There must have been fifteen or twenty up there from all the lead they threw down on us."

"There were four."

"Four? That's all?" O'Casey said, and gazed at the dead man. "More's the pity," he added softly.

"How many did we lose?" Fargo asked, nudging the Ovaro to move on up the line. The Irishman kept pace at his side. From behind and inside the wagons more troupe members appeared. Someone—it sounded like Briggs—shouted instructions.

"I haven't been able to make a count yet, but it was terrible," Kevin said. "They hit us before sunset, just as we came under that ridge. Two of the drivers and several horses were killed right then—"

"Horses pulling the first wagon," Fargo interrupted.

"Yes. How did you know?"

"They wanted to box you in. The trail is narrow here, with the river close by. There isn't enough room for a wagon to turn around. By stopping the first wagon they boxed in all of you."

"We were outsmarted by a bunch of savages," Kevin said bitterly.

"Never underestimate Indians. They can be as cagey as coyotes when they need to be."

Some of the acting company were making fires. Others were involved with gathering the horses. Still others were checking on the bodies or ministering to the wounded. By now they all knew what to do after an attack and everyone pitched in.

Skye reined up next to Molly's wagon and swung down just as three men came around the corner.

"Fargo! Thank God!" Tom Frederick exclaimed. "I'd about given you up for lost. Figured the Indians got you."

"They tried."

Pete stood on one side, Buffalo Briggs on the other. The wagon boss peered past the stallion.

"What's that you've got there? And where did those other horses come from?"

"I've brought meat. And those Indian horses can be ridden if you have men who don't mind going bareback."

"Meat!" Frederick cried, and ran to the pack animal. He touched the two deer as if he couldn't quite believe his own eyes. "Oh, Lord. This is too good to be true. After the work is done we'll have a feast."

"You'd be wise to ration the meat," Fargo advised. "There's no telling when I'll kill more. Give out enough tonight for everyone to have some decent stew, then smoke the rest."

"He makes sense," Briggs chimed in.

"All right," Frederick said, then turned hopeful eyes on the big man in buckskins. "Do you think you can kill more tomorrow?"

"I'll try, but I can't make any promises," Fargo said. He tied the Ovaro, then moved to the doorway. The door hung open and Molly wasn't inside. Turning, he scanned the vans but didn't see her.

"She's off helping the other women take care of those who were shot," O'Casey said at his elbow. "Want me to fetch her for you?"

"No. I'll see her later," Fargo replied. He closed the door, walked to the Ovaro, and led the stallion, the pack horse, and the Cheyenne mounts toward the river to let them drink before bedding them down for the night. Every muscle in his body ached. After riding all day, after hunting and fighting the war party, he was ready for a hot meal, steaming coffee, and a good night's sleep. But the Ovaro came first.

He raised his eyes to the stars filling the firmament and listened to the commotion at the wagons. The stallion and the pack horse drank greedily, while the Indian horses dipped their muzzles only now and then. Turning, he surveyed the vans, and movement at the wagon he shared with O'Casey and the others drew his attention.

Someone was slipping inside.

The door closed quickly, but not quickly enough to prevent him from recognizing Vangent. Now what was the teamster up to? Only one possibility occurred to him, and he hastily got the horses and took them to where the stock was being gathered.

Tyler, the youth who had almost shot him that day he stumbled on the wagon train, was walking by.

"Would you hold these horses for me?" Fargo asked, and before the youth could reply he handed them over and ran to the van. Gripping the latch firmly, he swiftly flung the door wide open and jumped up, filling the doorway.

The teamster was on his knees in front of an open closet, his hand buried in a piece of luggage belonging to Tom Frederick. He looked up, startled. "Fargo! I didn't expect you back so soon."

"Life is full of little surprises."

Vangent glanced down at the luggage and swiftly withdrew his hand. "Uhhh, I have a reason for being here."

"Don't waste your breath," Fargo said. "This is how you've done it."

"Done what?" the teamster said, standing, his manner that of a cornered rat that didn't know whether to flee or fight.

"How you've been able to search other wagons without being seen," Fargo said.

"I don't know what the hell you're talking about."

Fargo ignored his feigned innocence. "What are you looking for?"

"I'm not looking for nothing."

Placing his hands on his hips, Fargo took several steps nearer. He noticed a revolver tucked into the teamster's waistband, a Trantor, of all things. Trantors were relatively new, double-action, .43 caliber British revolvers more popular back in the East than in the West. Operatives of the Pinkerton Detective Agency were known to use them frequently because they were smaller than comparable Colts or Remingtons and could easily be concealed under jackets and coats. Smaller yes, but they packed plenty of stopping power. Where, he wondered, had the teamster obtained one? "I want the truth," he said.

Vangent's gaze dropped to the big .44 riding on the Trailsman's hip and he nervously gnawed on his lower lip.

"Don't try it," Fargo warned. "You'll be dead before that gun clears your belt."

"I believe you," Vangent said. "I saw you draw on Briggs. I wouldn't stand a prayer."

"Then why don't you take the gun and lay it on the closest bunk," Fargo directed. "Nice and slow, too. Don't do anything to give me the wrong idea."

"You won't get any argument from me," Vangent replied. Gingerly, his hand moving as slowly as a turtle stuck in mud, he used a thumb and forefinger to pull the Trantor out. Taking two steps, he carefully placed the revolver on a bottom bunk. "Will that do?" he asked, straightening.

"You did fine," Fargo said, allowing himself to relax. He'd expected Vangent to give him trouble, not to comply meekly. "Now we're going to have a talk with Tom Frederick."

115

"Whatever you say," Vangent said, and took a stride toward the door.

Shifting, Fargo motioned for the teamster to go first. In that instant, when he was turning and slightly off-balance, Vangent unexpectedly sprang and wrapped both arms around his midsection. The momentum lifted Fargo's boots from the floor, and before he could hope to react he found himself crashing onto his back near the entrance with the teamster on top.

Vangent was all business. He said nothing, made no threats. His fists spoke for him as he lashed out twice, a right and a left that both connected.

Fargo's head rocked with anguish as the teamster's granite-hard knuckles pounded onto his chin. His arms were pinned under Vangent, momentarily useless, but he was able to free his right leg and sweep his knee into the teamster's spine, and was gratified to see Vangent arch his back and grunt. A second kick caused Vangent to try and scramble to one side, but Fargo yanked his arms free, gripped the man by the front of his coat, and heaved as he drove both legs up and over.

The teamster sailed out the door like an oversized turkey, and with just as much flying ability.

Skye was on his feet and in the doorway in the blink of an eye. He saw Vangent rising slowly, dazed, and leaped, tackling Vangent around the knees and bearing them both to the ground. His right fist sank into the stocky man's gut and he followed through with a left to the head. Vangent went limp, and for a second Skye thought he'd won. He should have known better.

Teamsters and bull whackers were notorious for three things: their capacity to hold liquor, their tireless womanizing with the fallen doves of the saloons and houses of ill repute, and their readiness to brawl at the drop of a hat. No one ever beat a teamster easily.

Fargo, thinking Vangent had had enough, was starting to rise when a fist crashed into his left cheek and knocked him into the snow. Before he could regain his feet, Vangent rose and kicked him in the ribs. He doubled over and felt a second kick strike his lower back. Looking up, he found the teamster raising a boot to stomp him and promptly drove his legs into Vangent's and toppled the teamster on the spot.

Surging erect, Fargo raised his fists and bunched his shoulders. As Vangent came up, he was ready. He swung once, twice, three times, and each punch staggered his foe. Closing in, he swung again and again. Vangent might as well have been a tree for all the good it did. Then the teamster dug in roots and met Skye blow for blow.

Someone nearby was shouting angrily. Yells broke out along the line of wagons.

Fargo paid no attention. He dug in his heels and traded punches, giving as deftly as he got, perhaps better. There was formidable strength in the stocky teamster's blows. So was there strength in his. Twice he straightened Vangent like a board but the man refused to drop. They slugged furiously, both refusing to buckle, and they were still slugging a minute later when a shot rang out.

13

Vangent clutched at his chest, his wide eyes looking past Skye as if he couldn't believe what he saw. Then, in pitifully slow motion, he spun completely around and collapsed.

Fargo whirled. Off to one side stood Buffalo Briggs holding a smoking revolver. Over a dozen members of the troupe had gathered to witness the fight, and they were staring at the wagon boss with the same expression Vangent had worn. Fargo gripped his Colt but didn't draw. "What the hell did you do that for?"

"I figured you needed help," Briggs responded calmly, and placed the six-shooter in its holster.

Stepping to Vangent, Fargo knelt and felt for a pulse. There was none. "Damn you, Briggs. This wasn't necessary."

"I agree," stated Tom Frederick, stepping in front of the crowd. O'Casey, Pete, and Molly were right behind him.

"I was just doing my job, Mr. Frederick," Buffalo Briggs said. "You hired me to guide the wagons and protect all of you from whatever came along. Well, Vangent there was fixing to draw that knife up his sleeve and stab Fargo. I had to stop him, didn't I?"

"What knife?" Frederick said in surprise.

Briggs nodded at the body. "Up his left sleeve. Check, Fargo, and you'll see I'm right."

Knowing he would find one, Fargo pulled Vangent's left sleeve up above the wrist and displayed a dagger snug in a narrow leather sheath. At no time had he seen Vangent try to draw the blade. They had been going at it man to man, and he doubted the teamster would have resorted to the dagger unless Vangent felt his life was threatened.

"See? I told you," Buffalo Briggs said. "I knew he carried that hide-out, and I didn't want him sticking Fargo with it."

"Your concern for Fargo is commendable," Frederick said bitterly, "but your haste in shooting is reprehensible. The important point is that Vangent had no weapon in his hands when you callously shot him." He paused, scowling. "Mr. Briggs, I think your services are no longer required."

"What?"

Frederick faced Briggs. "Haven't I made myself sufficiently clear? As of this minute, your services are terminated."

"What?" Briggs said again, seemingly shocked by the news.

"You've been fired, mister. From now until we reach Miller's Crossing, Mr. Fargo will guide us. You may ride along, but in no way will you interfere in the day-to-day operation of this wagon train."

"You can't!" Briggs blurted, anger contorting his features. "You hired me for the duration. That was the deal."

"Do you remember that paper I had you sign?" Frederick asked coldly.

"The one with all the big words? I never bothered to read all of it."

"How unfortunate. Had you done so, you would know it is within my legal power as your employer to fire you at will. You're fired, and that's final."

Briggs took a half-pace toward Frederick, his fists balled, then changed his mind, wheeled on his heels, and stalked off.

"About time, I say," O'Casey commented.

While Fargo was glad to see Briggs get what he deserved, he wasn't pleased at having the responsibility for the entire company dropped in his lap without warning. Rising, he walked over to Frederick. "You could have waited until Denver."

"After what he just did? Never."

O'Casey motioned at several of the men. "Let's get to burying this one with the others. I'd like to get at least an hour's sleep this night."

"What's the final tally?" Fargo inquired.

"Four dead, three wounded," Frederick answered. "We lost seven horses as well. All in all, this trip has turned into a disaster of the first magnitude."

"It could have been worse."

"I don't see how."

"There could have been twice as many Indians and I might

never have shown up," Fargo said, and started off to take care of the Ovaro. Molly took hold of his arm as he passed.

"Will you stop and visit later?" she whispered.

"If you want the company."

"I've never needed it more."

Fargo nodded, then walked to where Tyler waited. Two large fires were blazing at opposite ends of the train, casting a yellowish glow over the surrounding snow. Shadows danced as if alive. He took the Ovaro and the Indian horses and tethered them. Unloading the pack horse, he let Tyler take care of it while he drew his toothpick and went to work on the deer and the rabbit.

As he mechanically cut and carved, he pondered the latest developments. Foremost was the reason Briggs had killed Vangent. Since the teamster had made no attempt to use the knife, Briggs had deliberately slain him to keep him from talking. So now Briggs was alone, unless there were accomplices on the train Fargo knew nothing of.

He recollected the horse tracks he'd seen on the trail after the blizzard and wondered if those riders had been trying to overtake the wagon train when the blizzard struck. If not for that blizzard, if not for Briggs losing his way and straying to the south, the quartet would surely have caught up with the vans days ago. It was an interesting train of thought.

By now those four should have reached Miller's Crossing if the Cheyennes hadn't gotten them first, which seemed unlikely since the war party had concentrated on the wagon train. If those four had reached the Crossing, they might still be there. Perhaps all the answers he wanted would be found there.

He worked silently except for the rustling of hide and the dripping of blood. First he placed each deer on its back. His razor-sharp knife made short shrift of slicing both deer from between their rear legs, up over their undersides, and as far up their necks as possible. He took turns going from deer to deer.

He had to be careful when cutting over the abdomen not to accidentally slice into the intestines or the stomach or he would contaminate the meat. The same held true for each windpipe and esophagus, which he had to sever close to the head and tie with a string to keep the contents from spilling out. He also cut each diaphragm muscle that separated the heart and lungs from the digestive tract. By the time he was done cutting inside, he was able to handily remove all of the internal organs simply by turning each animal on its side and letting the organs spill out.

Since the troupe was starved, there was no reason to hang each animal up to bleed. He picked up the rabbit and skinned it in no time flat. Then, spying Kevin walking toward him, he stood. "The meat is ready for the stew. But someone else will have to take care of smoking the rest. Does anyone know how?"

"I bet Buffalo Briggs does," the Irishman said with a grin. "And even though he no longer works for Mr. Frederick, he should still work to earn his keep. I'll ask him to do it."

Fargo squatted beside the buck. "I'll take some meat to Molly."

"Do you think we'll have any more trouble from those Cheyenne devils?" Kevin asked.

"No. But I could be wrong."

"No doubt about it, boyo. You are a wizard at inspiring a man with hope and confidence," Kevin said, and laughed.

Taking two sizable slabs of dripping meat, Fargo wiped the Arkansas toothpick clean on the buck's hide, slid the knife into his boot, and headed for Molly's wagon. His stomach rumbled the entire time. He could have eaten ten pounds of meat all by himself, but he had the troupe members to think of.

A pot rattled on the stove as he opened the door. Molly was preparing coffee. She glanced back and smiled. "How do you like your coffee? Weak as water? Or weaker?"

"Weak as water will do."

She saw the steaks. "Is all of that for us?"

"If I'm going to lead this outfit to Denver, I need to keep my strength up," Fargo said, and gave the meat to her. He moved to the washbowl in the corner, added water to it from the nearby pail, removed his hat, and washed his face and hands. Lacking a comb, he ran his fingers through his hair several times, then replaced his hat. When he turned, she had the coffee boiling and the steaks simmering, and the delicious aroma filled the wagon.

"I'm worried," Molly informed him. "Buffalo Briggs doesn't

121

impress me as being the forgiving kind. He might try to get back at you for being fired.''

Fargo had entertained the same notion. ''If he does, it will be his funeral.''

''You never cease to amaze me,'' Molly said earnestly. ''I've never met anyone so self-confident in all my life. Living off the land, living wild and free as you do, must make a man awfully self-reliant.''

''It teaches a man to know his limitations,'' Fargo said, stepping to a bunk and gratefully sitting down.

''I doubt you know the meaning of the word,'' Molly said.

Skye removed his coat and placed it on the bunk beside him. Then he propped his pillow against the wall and leaned back, his weary body aching from all he had been through since dawn. He idly watched Molly work at the stove, admiring the manner in which her hips swayed and her hair flowed when she moved. The delicious odor of the cooking food made his mouth water.

''Do you suppose there is a bathtub at Miller's Crossing?'' she asked, her attention on the steaks.

''I know there is. They have a big metal tub out back. Saw a man using it the last time I was there,'' Fargo told her.

''Outdoors? It's too cold to take a bath outside.''

''I bet Miller would lug it inside for you and set up blankets as curtains to keep out the curious.''

''What I wouldn't give for an hour in a hot tub,'' Molly said wistfully.

Fargo envisioned the sight and felt faint stirrings in his pants. ''I know old Miller pretty well. I can ask him for you when we get there.''

''You will not. A lady arranges her own baths, thank you very much. Miller might get the wrong idea if you were to ask him.''

Grinning, he waited impatiently for the food, and it wasn't too long before she brought over a sizzling steak on a plate. Next came a cup of hot, if weak, coffee. Like a starving wolf he tore into the venison, chewing and swallowing heartily. ''A man could grow fond of your cooking real fast,'' he said between mouthfuls.

''So you keep saying, but I doubt you'll be staying around

once we hit Denver,'' Molly said, taking a seat across from him, a plate in her left hand.

Skye paused with a forkful of juicy meat halfway to his mouth. "Why bring it up again? You know what will happen.''

She nodded. "You've been perfectly honest with me from the beginning. I dread the thought of not seeing you again, though. You're the first man I've opened up to in a long, long time.''

They ate in silence for a while. Fargo was aware of her probing stares but pretended not to notice. This had happened before with other women he'd known. Some women went to bed with a man and made more out of the love-making than it rightfully deserved. Many were lonely, like Molly, and they let their hearts get the better of their judgment and let their imaginations plant ideas better left alone. He didn't blame her for the way she was now feeling, but he didn't love her, either. Love took time to grow, to nurture like a little seed planted in fertile soil until it blossomed into a lasting romance. One passionate interlude hardly qualified as love. But he knew Molly had convinced herself she was in love with him, and he didn't relish hurting her feelings when it came time for them to take their separate trails.

"What are you thinking about?'' she asked when they were both almost done.

"Finding more deer tomorrow,'' Fargo fibbed.

She carried her empty plate to the table near the stove and set it down. "I was thinking about tonight. Must you turn in early?''

"I am tuckered out,'' Fargo said, grinning.

"I hope you're not too tired to move your lips,'' Molly replied, and came directly up to him, her body swinging suggestively, her slender hands on her hips.

This was the same woman who had been so reserved at first? Fargo took her into his arms and tilted her head to accept her fiery kiss. She darted her tongue deep into his mouth and he entwined his tongue with hers. Their lips remained glued together for minutes. All the while Fargo's hands roamed over her body, tracing the outline of her buttocks and the back of her smooth legs. He felt her full breasts and pressed a palm against her tummy. Her body reacted as if with a will of its own, mashing against him wherever he applied pressure. Between his legs his organ sprouted.

Molly took off his hat and dropped it on the end of the bunk. Her cool hands ran across his broad shoulders and along his sides. She breathed more heavily as time passed.

Fargo stood, brushing his body against hers, enjoying the way her legs parted slightly and her pubic mound thrust into his groin. She wanted him in the worst way, and her passion aroused him to extraordinary heights. His manhood pulsed with the urgency of his desire, but he restrained his need and savored every moment.

He nibbled on her ears and licked her neck. He cupped her posterior in his big palms and squeezed her as if her buttocks were melons being tested for ripeness. Her breathing grew heavier and heavier, and her lips seemed to be on fire.

He began undoing her clothing, forming a pile on the floor at their feet. The whole time, while at work removing a garment with one hand he would keep the other occupied with stroking her intimate parts. She quivered and cooed and ran her hand over the prominent bulge in his pants.

About that time he suddenly remembered that once again he hadn't locked the door. He was torn between the need for privacy and his hunger for her. To hell with it! he finally decided. He wasn't about to stop for any reason short of the end of the world, and if anyone made the mistake of entering without knocking first, he'd simply send whoever it was packing with a hail of lead.

Better yet, there was a lantern close at hand. He easily reached it with his left hand and extinguished the flame, plunging that corner of the van into relative darkness, enough to shield their activities should someone unexpectedly enter.

Soon he had her delightfully naked, and he relished the cool feel of her skin on his palms as he ran his hands over her pliant body. The tips of her breasts thrust upward, full and ripe for the kissing. His tongue swirled each one as she gripped the back of his head and puffed like a steam engine.

After finishing with her globes for the time being, he removed his shirt with one hand, then his gunbelt, boots, and pants. Their bodies were flush, skin to skin, his hard frame a sharp contrast to her soft contours.

Molly felt of his iron muscles and exhaled loudly. "You're exquisite. Do you know that?"

Instead of answering, Fargo traced his tongue from the base of her tender throat, down between her breasts, to just above her pubic hair. His nostrils registered the heady scent of her womanhood and he kissed her inner thighs.

"Ohhhhh, yes," Molly whispered. "You make me tingle all over."

A certain part of Skye's anatomy was also tingling to beat the band. He touched a palm to the junction of her legs and they parted to permit entry. Slowly, to tantalize her, he ran a single finger along the outer edge of her crack, and she shivered as if struck by a cold wind. She was moist and ready. He partially inserted his finger and she arched her back and lifted her left foot off the floor.

"Keep going," she whispered. "I can't stand the suspense."

He grinned wickedly and tantalized her further, running his finger back and forth but never penetrating into the depths of her slit. She shook and gasped and squeezed her thighs together. Then he stuck in another finger, and using the two as one he abruptly shoved them all the way into the core of her sex.

"Oh, God!" Molly shrieked, her nails biting into his back.

Fargo pumped his fingers slowly, building her toward a climax she would not soon forget. His fingers dripped with moisture. She bit him on the shoulder and the neck so hard it hurt.

"Yes! Like that!" she said between bites.

Withdrawing his hand, he scooped her into his arms and lowered her to the soft bunk, aligning himself between her willing legs. Again he inserted his fingers and stoked her furnace. She responded superbly.

The next moment he got a surprise. Her hands closed tenderly around his organ and lightly stroked it from top to bottom. A groan escaped his lips. He sat still as she played with him as he had played with her. A lump formed in his throat and he licked his lips in anticipation. When he could no longer stand it, he swooped his mouth to her nether lips.

"Do it! Do it!" Molly cried, bucking wildly.

Fargo had to hold onto her legs to keep her still enough to do what he wanted. His tongue probed and flicked and she became an inferno of desire, her fingers locked in his hair, her mouth a rosy oval. She panted heavily, her thighs shaking uncontrollably.

"I want you!" she said. "Oh, how I want you!"

The feeling was mutual, but Fargo wasn't about to rush. He licked until his tongue was sore and she was tugging on his hair to pull him out, and then he parted her legs wide, positioned his throbbing organ, and gave it to her.

Molly cried and gripped his upper arms, her nails digging deep. Her bottom rose to meet his paced thrusts. She licked her own lips, her eyes hooded, her breasts heaving.

It took all of Fargo's concentration to keep from spurting into her before he wanted to. He paced himself nicely, and not until she pleaded for him to bring her to the peak did he thrust himself all the way into her, his battering ram coated with the slick juices from her inner well.

"Aaaaaahhh!" Molly gasped. "Pound me, darling!"

He needed no more encouragement. He pounded and pounded until she gasped and clung to him and said his name a dozen times, and then he exploded with the force of a stick of dynamite.

Or so it seemed.

14

Miller's Crossing.

It came into view during the afternoon of the tenth day, and Fargo had rarely seen such a welcome sight as the large house, larger barn, and spacious corral, all in good shape. Smoke curled from the stone chimney Miller had built with his own hands. This was no rawhide outfit. Miller had picked this spot as the place where he would live out the rest of his days, and he built everything to last a lifetime. It showed.

The buildings sat on the north side of the Solomon River. To reach them, the river must first be crossed, but the water was invariably shallow at that point and posed no difficulty.

Fargo rode a dozen yards ahead of the lead van. He reined up at the water's edge and checked to make certain crossing would be easy. Then he motioned for the drivers to follow and let the Ovaro pick its way to the far side. The cold water only swirled to above the pinto's hoofs.

On the north side a gentle slope led up from the river. He stopped to watch the first two wagons enter the water, then turned and rode toward the house.

For the middle of winter, the place was exceptionally busy. There were ten horses in the corral and two more at a hitching post near the house. Beside the barn a Conestoga was parked. The barn doors were opened and a young man was busy forking hay to a horse in a stall. Another man and a woman were standing close to the front door, talking. At the west corner of the house lounged a lean man in buckskins who sported a black beard and a circular scar on his left cheek. He looked up, studied the vans for a moment, then hastened inside.

Isn't that interesting, Fargo reflected, making for the hitching post. The couple stared openly at him, smiling in a friendly fashion. From their attire he judged them to be farmers on their way west to the Promised Land, and he guessed they had arrived in the Conestoga. If they were traveling by themselves, they were fools, and he made a mental note to caution them later. He touched the brim of his hat in greeting. "Howdy, folks."

"Hello, friend," the man said, a sturdy sort in a heavy sheepskin coat who looked as if he could lift the front end of the Conestoga with one hand. "Have you had a long trip?"

"Longer than I liked," Fargo said, dismounting and tying the Ovaro to the post. The other two horses were sturdy bays, and from the tracks he gathered they had arrived only hours ago.

"My name is Swenson," the farmer stated. "This is my wife. We are bound for Oregon to make a new start."

"I wish you luck," Fargo said.

The young man who had been feeding hay to the horse in the barn came over, the pitchfork in his right hand. "Howdy, mister. Say, how many wagons you got there?" he asked, craning his neck to count them.

"Seven," Fargo answered, and grinned when the stable hand frowned. The man was thinking of all the extra horses he'd have to take care of. Skye stepped toward the door, intending to look up Tyson Miller. It suddenly opened and out came four men.

In the lead was a man unlike any other Fargo had ever laid eyes on. Tall, well over six feet, and endowed with wide shoulders and a slim waist, the man carried himself like a military officer. And well he should, because he was wearing a uniform with more gold trim and medals than any ten generals in the U.S. Army. White gloves covered his hands and a coat with a fur collar was draped over his shoulders. He wore a high, rounded hat secured by a chin strap. His green eyes, when they gazed at the train, were cold and appraising.

Behind him came two others similarly dressed, except this pair had fewer medals and little gold trim and were clearly inferior in rank.

The fourth man was the bearded man in buckskins.

Fargo stopped, his path blocked by the one with the gloves, and studied the four men closely before saying, "Excuse me. You're in my way."

"Go around," the big man said imperiously without so much as looking at Skye.

"I don't know where you hail from, mister, but out here it

isn't smart to be rude to strangers," Fargo said matter-of-factly. "You never know when they might up and shoot you full of holes."

The officer bestowed a look on Skye that would have withered a plant at ten feet. "Was that a threat, sir?"

Fargo grinned. "I wouldn't waste the lead. Now step aside."

"Do you have any idea whom you are addressing?"

"I don't care."

The man sniffed loudly. "I am Duke Francis von Metternick of Austria," he stated, his eyebrows trying to climb into his hat. "I am a special guest of the United States government, and I am conducting a tour of the West before I return to Austria."

"How nice," Fargo said dryly. Then suddenly he remembered. Metternick! That was the name of the man who had supplied Buffalo Briggs with a letter of reference. An idea occurred to him, and he abruptly pretended to be impressed. "Say. I have heard of you."

"Oh?" Metternick said, smiling smugly. Behind him, one at each elbow, were the other two soldiers. The man in the buckskins stood to one side, a quizzical expression on his scarred face.

"Yep," Fargo said, nodding. "I heard all about the letter of reference you gave to Briggs, the man I replaced." He waited, hoping for a reaction that might give some clue as to where Metternick stood in the scheme of things.

The duke reacted as if from a physical blow. His mouth slackened, his eyes widened, and his big hands formed into compact fists. He glanced at the approaching wagons, then at Skye. "Replaced, you say?" he said in a gravelly tone.

Fargo bobbed his chin. "Briggs was fired by Tom Frederick, the head of the Frederick Repertory Company. I've agreed to take them on to Denver."

Metternick scanned the area near the river. He stiffened, then shifted and barked instructions in an unfamiliar language to the two men with him.

Austrian, Fargo guessed, and watched the pair hasten past him. Just crossing the Solomon River was Buffalo Briggs, and he took one look at the twosome and reined up, frowning. This was becoming more interesting by the moment, Fargo reflected.

"If you will excuse me, sir," the duke said. He wheeled on his heels in a perfect about-face, then hurried into the house.

Fargo turned toward the bearded man in buckskins. "Hello, Larner."

The frontiersman gave a polite but curt nod. "Howdy, Fargo. I didn't think you'd recognize me."

"I've heard a lot about you," Fargo said, which was true. Around campfires at night and in every saloon west of the Mississippi many an hour was spent yarning about things of interest to travelers in the new, rugged land. Things like where the Indians were acting up, which trails were the safest to take, which lawmen were making a name for themselves, which towns boasted the best brothels, and which hardcases were best avoided at all costs. Larner fit into the last category.

"And I've heard tell about you," Larner mentioned, not sounding at all pleased that they had finally met face-to-face. "Shocked me seeing you come in with those folks."

"Why would that be?"

"I didn't know you was in this neck of the woods," Larner said.

"Same here," Fargo remarked. "Last I heard, you were up Oregon way robbing honest trappers of their hard-earned pelts."

Larner flushed. "That's a damn lie. Who told you that?"

"Jim Bridger, and he got it straight from a couple of old boys who had just come back from up there," Fargo said. He saw Larner hesitate. Even a renegade like him wasn't about to come out and label Jim Bridger a liar. Of all the mountain men, Bridger enjoyed an unequaled and highly deserved reputation for utter honesty and reliability.

"Well, those boys must have heard wrong themselves."

Fargo nodded at the doorway Metternick had just entered. "How'd you get hooked up with the likes of him?"

"I don't see where it's any of your damn business," Larner said, "but it just so happened I was in Kansas City when he advertised for a guide to take him to Denver." Spinning, he walked toward the barn, his shoulders square and stiff.

Skye reminded himself not to turn his back on that man or he might find a knife in it. He stepped onto the porch, kicked the snow and mud off his boots, and went in. The smell of cooking food drew him up short, and from a doorway on his left appeared a bear of a man in jeans and homespun shirt, his wrinkled bald head shining, his thick lips curling into a warm smile of greeting.

"As I live and breathe! If it ain't the Trailsman himself!"

"Hello, Miller," Fargo said, and shook hands. Old Miller might be well into his sixties, yet his grip was like a vise. "It's been a while."

"Too long, son. Too long. What brings you here at this time of the year?"

"I'm helping a bunch of actors reach Denver," Fargo said, and pointed at the window, where one of the large vans was visible as it moved toward the corral. "Seven wagons. And a bunch of starving people. I've been lucky and bagged deer practically every day, but they are hungry enough to eat your cupboard bare."

"Don't worry on that score, my friend. I have two root cellars crammed with enough food and supplies to outfit an army," Miller joked.

Fargo gazed beyond him to where the narrow hall broadened into a sort of lobby, an enormous room with a short bar on the west end, a half-dozen tables along the south wall next to the kitchen, and enough easy chairs, rockers and even a couch or two in the center to accommodate twenty people at one sitting. Everything Miller did, he did in a big way. Which was why Miller's Crossing was the favorite stopping place of many a weary traveler.

There were few people there at the moment. Over at the bar stood Duke Francis von Metternick, downing a drink as if it were to be his last. At a table sat two men in wide-brimmed hats and black frock coats, eating hungrily. Gamblers, from the looks of them.

Tyson Miller shifted to follow Fargo's gaze. "That gent at the bar fancies himself, I can tell you. He's from Europe. One of them royalties, to hear him brag on it." He paused. "We've also got a nice young couple heading for Oregon staying with us. I suppose you saw their Conestoga out front?"

"We met," Fargo said, and indicated the pair in frock coats. "What about them?"

"Gamblers on their way from Denver to Kansas City. Some kind of big poker tournament coming up in a few weeks in Kansas City and they're both planning to enter."

"Know their names?"

"Let me see," Miller said, and thoughtfully rubbed his chin. "One is called Gantry; the other is Hart. Can't remember which is which."

"Doesn't matter," Fargo said. He stretched and stared out the window at yet another wagon. The drivers had been instructed to take their wagons directly to the corral, where the horses would be tended to. Only then would the members of the troupe file into the way station.

"Are you expecting trouble?" Miller asked.

"Could be," Fargo said, and faced him. "Have you ever heard of a wagon boss named Buffalo Briggs?"

"Can't say that I have. Where did you run into him?"

"He'll be coming through this door in a bit. Between him, the duke over there, and Larner, this promises to be quite a stay."

"Hmmmm," Miller said. "I appreciate the warning. Now, why don't you get a bite to eat? You look peaked."

"Thanks. I will." Fargo ambled into the waiting room. The gamblers gave him searching stares and he nodded at them, then crossed to the bar. When the duke saw him coming, he put his glass down and made toward the stairs on the west side of the room.

"Leaving so soon?" Fargo asked. "I was hoping we could get acquainted."

"Perhaps another time," von Metternick said. He took the stairs two at a stride and disappeared when he reached the second floor.

Helping himself to a whiskey, Fargo leaned an elbow on the bar top. By all rights, considering everything he had been through to get the acting company safely to the Crossing, he should feel relieved and elated. He felt neither. Instead, the presence of the duke and Larner showed that the actors were far from being out of danger. There was still cause for concern. He intended to find out what those two were doing there, and he had no doubt they would be as cooperative as a nest of riled hornets.

He had a decision to make. Frederick wanted him to take the train all the way to Denver. He'd agreed to go as far as the Crossing, but now he must make up his mind whether to see the trip through to the end. Not that he had much choice. There was no one else capable of guiding them other than Larner, who was as trustworthy as a rabid wolf. And since there were women on the train, he couldn't very well turn Frederick down.

The troupe would stay at the Crossing for two or three days to allow the members time to rest and recover from their ordeal. Even more important, it would give the stock time to recuperate for the next leg of the journey. So Skye figured he had three days in which to unravel the mystery of Duke von Metternick and Buffalo Briggs.

There was a commotion near the entrance and the acting company trooped in, Tom Frederick and Kevin O'Casey in the lead. Miller appeared and welcomed them.

Finishing his drink, Skye watched the rest enter. Molly was walking with Abby, of all people, and the two were talking as if they were the best of friends. The entire troupe spread out among the tables and took seats. A good meal was the first thing on their minds.

Fargo waited, but no one else came in. What had happened to Buffalo Briggs? And where were the two soldiers who had been with the duke? He waited another minute, then made for the front door.

"Skye! Care to join us?" Molly asked.

"Maybe in a few minutes," Fargo replied. "Have something to do right now."

The bright sun made him squint when he stepped outside. The air was warm, the snow in the yard almost completely melted. Near the barn the stable worker was busy taking the horses out of their harnesses and leading the animals into the corral. He shifted and spied Briggs's dun on the north side of the barn, just standing there with its head drooping and its reins dragging.

Loosening the Colt in his holster, Fargo moved toward the corner of the barn. Off to the south, near the river, was the couple headed for Oregon. No one else was around. Not Briggs, and not the two beefy military men. Slowing, he came to the corner and stopped. He could hear the horse breathing, nothing else.

"Can I help you, mister?"

The shout brought Fargo around quickly, a scowl of annoyance creasing his brow. The stable hand, who had started in his direction, halted just as quickly.

"I don't want no trouble, mister. I figured you might be looking for me," the man said.

"Did you see other men come this way? A man from the wagon train and two soldiers?"

"You mean those dudes in the fancy uniforms? I took them for a bunch of danged foreigners."

"Did you see them?" Fargo asked, every word clipped and precise.

The stable hand blinked, then glanced at the .44. "No, sir, I did not. I've been busy with this stock." He ventured a wan smile and went back to work.

Struggling to control his irritation, Fargo peeked around the corner but saw only the horse. If there had been anyone nearby, he would have headed for cover when the stable hand shouted. He stepped forward warily, studying the ground, and found plenty of tracks. Too many. It looked as if a half-dozen head of cattle had drifted past the spot not more than thirty minutes ago, and their heavy hoofs had made a mess of the mud. It was almost impossible to distinguish other prints, but he found where three sets of boot prints moved away from the dun and toward the rear of the barn.

He trailed them, halting at the far corner to check what lay beyond. There was a narrow field, then a low knoll. The cattle were spread out across the field, one nibbling on the tips of a bush and the rest either chewing their cuds or gazing into the distance.

The boot prints led to the base of the knoll.

Puzzled, Fargo advanced, his arm tensed, ready to draw should he spy the glimmer of sunlight off a gun barrel. From the tracks, he knew Briggs had been between the two Austrians, who wore larger boots and were twenty to thirty pounds heavier. They must be somewhere up ahead, perhaps on the other side of the knoll.

His prediction proved accurate. When he came to the base, he saw where the trail led up and over. Now he was even more they had talked, he'd learned that the Austrian was pompous and arrogant. Now he must add deadly to the list. Metternick was a man accustomed to having his own way at all times, a high-ranking military man who only had to open his mouth and others would do his bidding. Like those two beefy soldiers.

Straightening, Fargo debated whether to inform Miller of the death. If he did, Miller, or more likely Miller's wife, might be tempted to send word to the nearest fort or to contact the closest federal marshal. Should that happen, the duke and his men might ride off before the authorities arrived to avoid being questioned. He concluded he would keep his mouth shut. If the Austrians believed the body had not been discovered, if they believed they were free to do as they pleased, they might become careless and give him a clue as to what was going on.

Above all else, Fargo wanted to get to the bottom of the mystery. So far four people had died because of it. If he counted in all the lives taken by the Cheyenne war party, the toll was much higher. Indirectly, the affair was possibly to blame there, too. The troupe would not have been in the wrong place at the wrong time if not for Briggs, and Briggs was linked somehow to the duke.

The duke.

All the trails of Fargo's thoughts led to the same source; Duke Francis von Metternick of Austria. Metternick had all the answers, of that Fargo was convinced. And somehow he must uncover them before any more members of the troupe died or the Austrians did to him what they'd done to Buffalo Briggs.

Holding the Colt steady, he followed the boot tracks of the two soldiers into the brush. They had made no effort to conceal their footprints, which showed them to be tenderfeet in one respect. After forcing their way through a thicket, they had followed a rabbit run in the general direction of the station.

Soon Fargo found himself twenty yards to the rear of the house. The trail led out of the brush and past the outhouse, where the boot prints of the Austrians were lost in the maze of tracks between the outhouse and the house proper. Clever, Fargo reflected, but not clever enough.

He slid the .44 into its holster, adjusted his hat, and went in the back door. A hallway led toward the large room at the front, passing a number of rooms along the way. From his past visits he knew the back section and the entire upstairs were devoted to rooms for those staying over. Nice rooms, too, with comfortable beds and mirrors in every one.

The main room bustled with activity. The actors and actresses were busily eating their fill. Both gamblers stood near the bar, drinking. The farmer and his wife were seated on a couch, holding hands. There was no sign of the Austrians.

Fargo walked over to the table where Molly and Abby sat. "That offer to join you still open?"

Molly glanced up and smiled. "It certainly is. We're about done, but I'd love your company."

"We had beef and eggs and they were delicious," Abby told him.

"Then I'll have the same," Fargo said. He spied Mrs. Miller moving among the tables and called out to her. She came right over, he placed his order, and she departed.

"Isn't this place magnificent?" Molly said, gazing in awe at the massive beams above them. "I can't get over finding such a fine house out here in the middle of nowhere."

"You'd be surprised at the folks you find living in the most out-of-the-way spots," Fargo said, staring at the stairs. A few actors were drifting up to their rooms.

"Tom Frederick says he'd like to stay here three days," Molly said. "Is that all right with you?"

"Fine," Fargo said absently. He suddenly remembered that he'd left the Ovaro at the hitching post. After the meal he must bed it down.

"Speak of the devil," Abby said.

Frederick, O'Casey, and Pete were walking toward them. Frederick got right down to business.

"Have you seen Buffalo Briggs? We haven't found anyone who recalls seeing him after we arrived."

"What's the problem?" Fargo inquired.

"I've been talking to Miller. He says he's either met or heard about every wagon boss who takes trains from Kansas City to Denver, and he's never heard of Briggs. Never heard of Webster Pass, either, or of any Indian named Chief Gray Wolf." He frowned. "You were right, Fargo. Briggs was a complete and so hostile there at the beginning. The duke undoubtedly paid Briggs handsomely to carry out his wishes. Briggs must have been furious at being thwarted.

Then, once the attempt on Skye's life had failed and Briggs realized he couldn't get rid of him, the man had become downright friendly. Maybe Briggs had been trying to divert any suspicions Skye might have entertained. Maybe the subsequent searches of the wagons had been a last resort to locate whatever the duke was after.

Fargo stopped chewing and leaned back in his chair. Suddenly it all seemed so clear. Or was he deluding himself and letting his imagination fill in the gaps with wild guesses? The only man who could answer that question was upstairs.

"Are you sure you're all right?" Molly asked.

"Fine," Fargo replied. He chatted about the weather and the trail between Miller's Crossing and Denver while he finished his meal. Most of the troupe had downed theirs by the time he was done eating and had gathered near the bar. Even those who rarely drank were enjoying the opportunity to mingle and talk.

"Abby wants to share a room with me," Molly told Fargo, and frowned. "It doesn't appear as if we'll find time to be together for the next three days."

"It's a long way to Denver," Fargo said. He grinned, winked, and pushed back from the table. "I've got to take care of my horse. How about if I join you for a drink later?"

"I'll be waiting."

Rising, Skye walked to the entrance and stepped outside to find the sun hovering above the western horizon. The stable hand was taking harness into the barn to hang it up. No one else was around. He untied the Ovaro and led the stallion to the wide open door.

The hired hand glanced around at the sound of the Ovaro's hoofs. "Oh. It's you. You can put your horse in the corral with the rest."

"I want a stall."

"Costs extra."

"A stall," Fargo stressed, entering.

Pointing at an empty one on the south side of the barn, the hand said testily, "There's one you can have. I'll get around to stripping your saddle and feeding your horse as soon as I'm done with the other stock.''

"I'll take care of my own horse," Fargo said, moving down the central aisle.

"You will?" the hand said, then smiled. "Fine, mister. There's plenty of hay in the loft and oats in a bin over yonder. Help yourself."

"I will. Thanks."

"If you need anything else, give a yell," the hand said, and hastened out, pleased he was getting out of doing some work.

It took over half an hour for Fargo to strip off his saddle, rub down the Ovaro, and feed it. He took his time, thinking over what to do about the duke. When he was done, he went to the door and looked for the stable hand. The man was just going into the house. Instantly Fargo hastened around the corner and spied Briggs's horse thirty feet away, its reins tangled in a bush.

With a glance at the house to make certain no one was watching, Fargo jogged to the dun, unfastened the reins, and took the animal into the barn. He removed the saddle and blanket, hung them on a rail, and led the dun into the corral where the other horses were feeding. Now, if anyone came searching for Briggs's mount, he'd find it right where it should be.

What about the body? Fargo asked himself. Someone might go out to gather the cattle, spy the tracks, and follow them. He should conceal the corpse until later. Pivoting on his boot heels, he hurried across the field to the knoll and climbed to the top. The sun was almost gone and twilight enveloped the land. A cool breeze from the northwest stirred his hair. He looked down, then froze in surprise.

The body was gone.

Running to the spot, he saw where someone had come along and dragged Briggs into the brush to the south. The drag marks were as plain as day. He followed them, trying to tell from the prints who might have done the deed. Had the duke sent one of the officers to hide the body? He came to the brush and sank to his left knee so he could examine the ground carefully. His head bowed, he traced a partial print with his fingers.

To his left, something rustled.

Fargo detected motion out of the corner of his eye and dived forward. A heavy object struck him a glancing blow on the side of the head, dazing him. He landed on his stomach and had the presence of mind to roll in case his attacker cut loose with a gun. Feeling slightly dizzy, his vision fuzzy, he pushed to his knees, his right hand palming the Colt in a smooth, practiced draw. But as he brought the revolver clear there was a glimmer of light and something struck the barrel hard, hard enough to knock the .44 from his hand. He surged upright, gritting his teeth and trying to focus.

His vision suddenly cleared, and there before him was Con Larner hefting a Crow tomahawk. He looked around for the Colt but failed to find it.

"Something the matter, Fargo?" Larner baited him. "Where's all that grit I hear you have?"

Skye held himself poised to evade another swing. If he could only grab the Arkansas toothpick! But Larner would swing the instant he doubled over to reach into his boot.

"Your meddling has made the duke very unhappy," Larner said, inching to the right.

"What's he after, Con?" Fargo asked, stalling for time so he could think and recover from the swipe to the skull. He glued his eyes to that tomahawk, knowing Larner could use it as deftly as any Indian.

"You don't know?" Larner said, and gave a contemptuous snort. "And here I heard you were supposed to be so all-fired smart."

The tomahawk arced at Skye's face and he swiftly back-pedaled. His second step brought his spine up against the thicket, and he had to dart to the right to avoid being split open by another swing. Retreating farther, he inadvertently backed into a pocket in the thicket and became hemmed in on three sides of the slender, jagged branches.

"Not very bright," Larner said, smirking. He wagged his tomahawk and made a threatening gesture but didn't press his attack. "Wait until the word gets out that I killed you! Some of your old enemies will be glad to hear the news."

"You're counting your chickens before they're hatched,"

Fargo said, continuing to watch the tomahawk. When the move came he must be ready.

"No one has ever beaten me at hand-to-hand fighting," Larner boasted. "Why do you think I've got the reputation I do?"

"Because you've bushwhacked a lot of unsuspecting people."

Larner's features hardened. "You think you know everything, but you don't. Hell, you don't even know about the Neustadt emeralds."

"Is that what the duke is after?"

Scowling, Larner came in with a rush, the tomahawk descending from on high to split Fargo's skull. Only this time Skye was prepared. He slid in close, under the swing, and gripped the arm holding the tomahawk in both hands. Without missing a heartbeat, he whirled while yanking down hard on Larner's forearm.

Larner left his feet like a bird taking off. He sailed clean over Fargo's head and crashed into the thicket. A yelp of pain greeted his landing, and for a moment he lay flat on his back, stunned.

Fargo stooped, pulled the toothpick out, and sprang forward. He had the advantage. Now he would make Larner talk. But the brutal killer recovered in a twinkling and lashed out with a leg. Fargo felt the heel of Larner's foot smash into his shin, and then he toppled, sprawling to the ground on Larner's left. He pressed his palms down, about to heave to his feet, and looked at Larner. Just as the tomahawk streaked at his face.

16

Larner, lying on his side, swung awkwardly, unable to get his full force behind the swing.

Reacting instinctively, knowing he couldn't hope to push away in time, Fargo took a grave chance and hurled himself at Larner instead. His left elbow deflected the arm swinging the tomahawk, and then they were nose to nose, Larner's hand on his right wrist to keep him from sinking the toothpick into Larner's body, while Fargo's left hand held the arm holding the tomahawk at bay. They grappled, each striving his utmost to break free, rolling over and over, crashing into bushes where their faces and hands were gouged and cut by thin limbs.

Fargo was surprised at Larner's strength. Although smaller and thinner, Larner possessed the strength of a mountain lion and the sinewy speed of one of the big cats. Hatred glared from Larner's eyes and his lips were curled up over his clenched teeth as he hissed and grunted.

The contest waged for over a minute with neither man gaining a decisive edge.

Thrashing and rolling as they were, Fargo lost all sense of direction and had no idea where they were in relation to the thicket until they smashed into it. Repeatedly. Once a limb opened a gash under his left eye, almost blinding him.

He rolled into a heavy bush yet again, with Larner on top. Inspiration sparked action. Uncoiling his legs, he flipped Larner up and over, headfirst into the thicket, then leaped to his feet.

Larner vented an inarticulate cry. He got to his knees, stood, and backed up, his left hand pressed over his eyes. "No!" he raged, and spun.

Fargo saw blood trickling from under Larner's palm, and when the man moved his hand he saw the reason why. Both eyes had been punctured, the left worse than the right. They were watering and rimmed with blood. Larner blinked frantically in an effort to clear them and eventually succeeded to an extent, because he moved toward Fargo, tomahawk raised.

"You bastard!" he roared, and stepped closer, swinging purposefully.

Ducking under the swipe, Fargo speared the toothpick into Larner's chest. Larner stiffened, then tottered backward, his lips moving soundlessly. His motion caused the slender knife to slip out of his body followed by a fine crimson spray. Staggering, Larner tried to turn, as if to flee, but his legs gave out and he sank to his knees.

"This can't be," he muttered. "This can't be."

Fargo said nothing. He wiped the knife clean on the trampled snow underfoot, then held it ready to use again.

Wheezing, Larner dropped the tomahawk and gingerly touched the hole in his chest. "Oh, no," he moaned, and looked blankly around. "Fargo? Are you there?"

"I'm here."

Larner shifted. "You've done me proper, mister. I never figured on this." He coughed up blood and doubled over.

"You brought this on yourself," Skye said grimly.

For a space Larner did nothing but cough, his body shaking uncontrollably. Then he regained control and lifted his head. "I reckon so," he said softly.

Fargo took a half-step closer. He didn't like to see anyone suffer, even an enemy. If there was fighting to do, his philosophy was to do what had to be done and get it over with as quickly as possible. Many Indian tribes inflicted torture on their enemies, but he didn't believe in the practice. If a man needed killing, then the son of a bitch should be killed and that was that. "I can put you out of your misery," he offered.

Larner inhaled deeply. "No. Thanks." He paused to cough. "But there is something you can do for me."

"Why should I?"

The answer came in spurts as Larner gathered breath time and again. "Because you're not one of those no-account pilgrims from back in the States . . . whether you want to admit it or not, you're a lot like me . . . we've taken different trails, but we've both traveled far and wide in our time."

"I owe you nothing."

Larner craned his neck, his face adopting a plaintive expression. "Please, Fargo. I have a sister in St. Louis. Name of Harriet Larner. She don't have much." He stopped and bent low, groaning.

Fargo glanced around. They were a good ten feet into the underbrush and no one else had shown up. He knew no one at the house could have heard the scuffle, which was probably why Larner had used the tomahawk instead of a gun. Then Larner moaned and spoke again.

"There's two hundred dollars in my pocket. My advance from the duke. Mail it to my sister the first chance you get."

"How do you know I won't keep it?"

A wry grin curled Larner's lips. "Hell, everyone knows you're as good as your word. If you tell me you'll mail it, I know she'll get it."

"All right," Skye said. "I'll mail the money on one condition."

"What?"

"Tell me everything you know about the duke."

More coughing, the most violent yet, delayed Larner's reply. At last he raised his head a bit and mustered the strength to whisper. "Don't know a whole hell of a lot. He's after those emeralds. Worth a fortune, I was told. His government needs 'em."

"Who has them?"

"That's just it. He doesn't know for sure. Someone with the . . . the . . ." Larner said, and gasped. A single tiny gasp, then he pitched onto his face and was still, his arms going limp at his sides.

"Damn," Fargo muttered. He knelt, searched for the money, and found a poke that he quickly pocketed. "Harriet Larner," he said to himself, then went to Buffalo Briggs's body and dragged it into the thicket, where he placed it next to Larner's. He was about to depart when a thought hit him. Crouching, he searched Briggs's pockets and found two hundred dollars in new gold coins in one of them. The duke, evidently, was free with his money.

He stuck Briggs's coins into his own pocket and stood. The sun was down, the sky growing rapidly darker. Wheeling, he hurried to the station. He didn't want Molly or anyone else to miss him and come looking. Nor did he want to bump into the Austrians until he had a few more answers. Then it would be time to tangle with them.

Now he knew the reason the duke had arranged for Briggs to become the wagon boss. He didn't know where Metternick had found Briggs, but it was obvious the duke had paid Briggs to pose as a seasoned wagon boss and to guide the wagons to a spot where the duke could ransack the wagon train at his leisure and find the emeralds. The blizzard had ruined the duke's well-laid plans.

Briggs had probably had Vangent search the wagons on his own initiative. When Vangent had been caught, Briggs had shot him to keep him from talking. In the end, Briggs had paid dearly for his treachery and lies.

But who had the emeralds? Where did the emeralds come from? Why did the Austrian government want them so badly? If he knew the answers to all of these questions, he'd know why Metternick had traveled to America and gone to so much trouble to lay his hands on the precious gems.

The stable hand was nowhere around, and no one was strolling about in the cool air. He went into the barn, removed his Sharps from the saddle scabbard, then entered the house through the front door.

Tyson Miller stood in a doorway on the left, conversing with the stable hand. He took one look at Fargo and came over. "Good Lord, man. What happened to you?"

"What do you mean?"

"Your face. Have you been wrestling a wolverine?" Miller asked, and indicated a mirror on the wall.

Thin red streaks crisscrossed Skye's cheeks. There was the nasty gash under his left eye and another on his right ear. He wiped his sleeve across his face, but it did little more than smear the blood.

"Here," Miller said, opening a door. "There's a washbowl with fresh water and a towel you can use." He stood aside so Fargo could go into the small room. "Care to tell me about it?"

Fargo leaned the Sharps against the wall, dipped his big hands in the bowl, and splashed refreshingly cool water on his cheeks.

Since the killings had been committed on Miller's property, Miller had a right to know. But he didn't want the word out just yet. Not until he had settled accounts with Duke von Metternick. "As soon as I can I'll fill you in."

"Is the other gent worse off then you?"

"Much worse."

"Uh-oh," Miller said. "I'd better keep my shotgun handy tonight, just in case."

"You do that," Fargo responded, and rubbed the towel on his face. Grabbing the Sharps, he checked himself in the mirror. The cuts were barely visible and there was no blood. He was presentable. Holding the rifle in the crook of his left arm, he walked into the main room, intent on wetting his whistle. But the sight of the tall man in uniform seated in an easy chair with a ring of attentive listeners drew him up short.

Duke Francis von Metternick himself. Behind him, discreetly standing with their hands clasped behind their broad backs, were the two subordinate officers.

Fargo drifted closer, keeping in back of others so the duke wouldn't catch sight of him. He noticed Molly and Abby near the front of the listeners. The duke was addressing the crowd.

" . . . having a marvelous time in your wonderful country. It is so unlike my beloved Austria as to be a different world. The emperor will not believe my tales when I get back."

"Oh!" Abby exclaimed. "You know an emperor?"

The duke displayed all of his perfect teeth. "My dear lady, I am one of his personal advisors. But let me add, there isn't a king or prince or anyone of note in all of Europe whom I have not met."

"My, you must live an exciting life," Abby cooed.

"You have no idea," Metternick said.

Kevin O'Casey, who had his arms folded across his chest, lowered them and said, "Excuse me, sir. But perhaps you can clear a confusing matter up for me?"

"If I can," the duke replied.

"I was reading a newspaper in Chicago some time ago, and I distinctly recall seeing an article about a war in your country. Something about the French and Sardinians beating your army and taking some of your territory."

Metternick's eyes narrowed. "True, sir," he replied bitterly. "But I can assure you they would not have won had not a traitor in our ranks provided them with critical information on the placement of our troops."

"And now your country is beset by insurrections," O'Casey said. "It seems to me Austria must be a very unhealthy place for its rulers at the moment."

The duke cocked his head and regarded O'Casey coolly. "You are remarkably well informed for an American. Might I ask your name?"

"Kevin O'Casey, at your service."

"An Irishman, are you not?"

"Yes," Kevin confirmed proudly.

"How interesting," Metternick said, his brow creasing in thought.

Abby leaned forwad. "Duke, tell us more about the royal court. I'd love to hear more about that prince you were telling us about earlier."

Fargo hefted his rifle, debating whether to confront Metternick. Suddenly his attention was drawn to Kevin O'Casey, who had moved away from the group and was quickly and quietly making for the entrance. The Irishman cast an apprehensive glance over his shoulder, then rounded the corner.

Curious, Fargo followed. The sky was dark, the air crisp. He saw Kevin hurrying into the barn and ran to the open door. Kevin had lit a lantern and was preoccupied with putting a saddle on a bay in one of the stalls.

"Going somewhere?" Fargo asked.

Kevin jumped and spun around, his right hand going to his chest. "Damn, boyo! Don't be sneaking up on a man like that. You about gave me a heart attack."

"It's a bit late in the day for a ride," Skye remarked, walking to the stall.

"I was restless and wanted some exercise," Kevin said. He turned and began cinching up.

"Is that the real reason?" Fargo asked.

"Of course. What else?"

"It could be you're running from the duke."

Kevin became stone. He took a deep breath and faced around. "What do you know?"

"Not enough," Fargo admitted. "I know the duke is after some emeralds. And I know he's willing to kill anyone to get his hands on them. He had Briggs killed—"

"Briggs is dead?" Kevin exclaimed, aghast.

"And the duke sent Con Larner after me. Larner used a tomahawk, thinking he could make it look like Indians had done the job. But he wasn't up to it."

"Begorra!" Kevin breathed, and leaned on the saddle. "Is there no end to the madness?"

"Tell me everything you know," Skye said.

"I don't have the time," Kevin answered, grabbing a bridle from a peg on the wall. "The duke is on to me now. I was a fool. Should have kept my fool mouth shut and not sounded him out. He noticed my brogue right away. And here I thought I'd about eliminated it."

Fargo placed a restraining hand on the Irishman's shoulder. "Forget the bridle. Where are you going to go in the middle of the plains in the dead of winter?"

"I'll try to reach Denver."

"By yourself? You'll never make it."

Kevin jerked his shoulder away. "It's either that or stay here and wait for the duke and his bullyboys to get their mitts on me. If they do, I'm dead."

"Why would they come after you? Do you know where the emeralds are?"

Kevin bit his lower lip in his anxiety, then nodded. "I'm the only one who does. And they'll torture me to get at the truth." He bowed his head. "I'm not sure I could keep my mouth shut."

"Where are the emeralds?"

The Irishman glanced up. "The less you know, the better. If I die, the secret of where the emeralds are hidden dies with me. That filthy Metternick will never get his hands on them."

"Why does he want them?"

"You don't know? The Neustadt emeralds are worth a fortune, boyo. Over one hundred and ten million dollars. Money like that could buy a lot of arms and supplies for the Austrian army."

"The Austrian government plans to sell them?" Fargo asked.

"So my brother heard. The war against the French and Sardinians drained the Austrian treasury, so the government has taken to selling off gems and paintings and the like to raise money for their army. If they get enough money they'll be able to crush the insurrections.''

"How do you know all this?"

"My brother," Kevin said, and sighed. "My parents had nine children in all. I was the first-born. Seven of us are boys and we're a traveling brood. One of my younger brothers took to gallivanting all over Europe and married an Austrian woman. He stayed there so she could be close to her family. Over the years he's written quite a few letters and told me about how harsh and oppressive the government is.''

The Irishman stopped and Fargo waited patiently.

"His wife's father became involved with the opposition. The movement bombs Austrian military posts, assassinates government officials, and causes general mayhem. A while back they learned the government planned to sell off some of the treasures in the national museum.''

Skye heard the wind intensify outside. It howled past the barn and off across the yard.

"So the rebels broke into the museum and stole whatever they could get their hands on," Kevin went on. "Including the emeralds. The government offered a huge reward for information and an informer gave them names of top rebel leaders. My brother's father-in-law was arrested.''

The Ovaro whinnied but Fargo paid little attention. He was too interested in the tale O'Casey was telling.

"My brother's wife wound up with the emeralds. He knew the soldiers would come after them, knew they had no hope of getting out of the country safely, so he did the only thing he could think of.''

Fargo guessed what that had been. "Your brother sent the emeralds to you.''

"Hidden in a cigar box with a note to hold onto them until I heard from him or someone in the rebel movement," Kevin confirmed. "But it's been many weeks and I haven't heard from him. I fear he's in prison or dead.''

Fargo didn't say anything. Since the duke was in America, the Austrians obviously knew where the emeralds had been sent. And the only way they could have found out was from Kevin's brother or the brother's wife.

"I know Metternick is after the emeralds," Kevin commented. "But I don't understand why he didn't come after me at the beginning instead of killing Wehner and Schweer."

"Perhaps I can explain, gentlemen," stated a stern voice to their rear.

Skye pivoted, starting to level the rifle, but he was far too late. Standing in the doorway was Duke Francis von Metternick and the two officers, all three with revolvers trained either on O'Casey or him.

The duke smiled. "One move, gentlemen, and you die."

17

"I knew I should have rode off," Kevin said.

The three Austrians came into the barn and the duke barked orders to one of his men, who promptly swung the large doors closed.

"We wouldn't want to be disturbed, would we?" Metternick said.

Fargo was calculating his chances of cutting loose and downing all three before they got him. The odds weren't favorable. He might kill the duke and one of the junior officers, but the third man would surely nail him.

Again the duke gave orders; and the same man who had closed the doors walked around behind Skye and gingerly divested him of his hardware. Then the officer moved back to stand beside the duke.

"That's better," Metternick said, relieved. "Now that I need not worry about you trying to shoot me, Mr. Fargo, we can discuss the situation like rational adults."

"We have nothing to talk about, you murderous butcher!" Kevin snapped.

"Ah, but we do," the duke countered. "I didn't hear all of your conversation, but I heard enough to know that you are the man I have been seeking, Mr. O'Casey." He took a step forward. "Where are the emeralds?"

"Go to hell."

"You will precede me, I'm afraid, unless you tell me where I can find the emeralds. My government needs them, and I have promised to return them to Vienna or never show my face in my beloved country again."

Kevin smiled tightly. "Then you will be an outcast the rest of your days."

"I think not," Metternick said, and glanced at Fargo. "Do you know where the emeralds are?"

Before Skye could answer, Kevin O'Casey declared angrily, "No, he doesn't. I'm the only one who does."

"So," the duke said, extending his gun toward Kevin. "It is between us, then. Although I must confess I do not know how you fit into this affair." He pursed his lips. "Do you know a man named William Kilmacthomas?"

"He is my brother," Kevin said.

"But you said your name is O'Casey," Metternick noted.

"My stage name is O'Casey. I adopted it when I took up the acting profession."

Duke Francis von Metternick threw back his head and laughed. "So that's it! I went to all this trouble because of a stage name!" He saw the confusion on Fargo's face and clucked. "You see, Mr. Fargo, when we searched William Kilmacthomas's house we found pieces of charred paper in the fireplace. He'd burned a draft of a letter he'd written, but we recovered enough to learn important clues. The heading was still legible, so we knew it had been sent to the Frederick Repertory Troupe of Chicago."

Fargo saw one of the officers turn to the door and tilt his head as if listening.

"Since we did not find the emeralds on Kilmacthomas or in his house before he died, I deduced he'd sent them to someone associated with the acting company," Metternick went on.

"Bill is dead?" Kevin said bleakly.

"Yes, and it was an unnecessary death. All he had to do was tell us where to find the gems," Metternick replied. "There has been one unnecessary death after another since this miserable affair began. Wehner was killed because he was working late and saw my men searching the theater where the troupe was performing."

"And Schweer?" Kevin asked bitterly.

"Buffalo Briggs heard Schweer say he'd been to Europe, so Briggs assumed Schweer must be the man I was after. He tried to question Schweer but in the process killed him," the duke said, and scowled. "Briggs was a fool. I should never have hired him to guide your wagon train."

The officer who had been listening at the door suddenly whispered in German. Instantly the duke and the second officer

155

moved to one side where they wouldn't be seen should the door open.

A moment later it did, and Molly walked in, a shawl draped over her shoulders. "Skye! Here you are," she said, and then gasped as the first officer, who had pressed himself against the wall, stepped forward and covered her with his gun.

Duke von Metternick strolled into the open. "This is most unfortunate, my dear. Is anyone else coming?"

"No," Molly said, then added almost in the same breath, "What is all this? Why are you holding guns?"

"I'm afraid I don't have time to provide answers," Metternick told her. "We must leave before others decide to join our little party." He issued instructions to his men and they holstered their sidearms and set about saddling horses.

This was the moment Fargo had been waiting for. He inched toward Metternick, but the duke wagged a finger at him.

"Behave yourself, Mr. Fargo, or this lovely lady dies." So saying, Metternick touched the tip of his gun barrel to Molly's temple.

Frustrated by his helplessness, Fargo controlled himself as six horses were prepared. He held no illusions about the duke's next step. Metternick would take them far enough away from the station so that shots or screams couldn't be heard, and then he would have Molly and him shot or stabbed. Afterward, Kevin would be subjected to excruciating torture until he revealed the location of the emeralds.

When the horses were all saddled the two subordinates drew their revolvers again and stood by while Fargo, Kevin, and Molly mounted, Fargo astride the Ovaro. Then the duke stepped onto a horse and covered Molly while his men opened the wide doors.

Lanterns had been lit in the house and the glare from the windows formed squares of light on the snow and mud. Partially drawn curtains concealed the occupants and prevented anyone inside from observing the activity at the barn.

"Head due west," Metternick ordered.

The Austrians might be greenhorns where the West was concerned, but they were no-nonsense military men whose lives were dedicated to self-discipline and fighting. They knew how to handle prisoners. The two subordinates rode on either side while the duke brought up the rear, right behind Molly.

For Fargo, the temptation to make a break was almost irresistible. They crossed the field and skirted the knoll. He had only to spur the Ovaro and cut into the brush and he would be in the clear. He didn't do it. He couldn't escape while Molly and Kevin were still in danger. There had to be another way.

A sliver of moon afforded scant illumination. Much of the snow had melted and they rode over alternate tracts of mud and soft white mush.

In the lead, Fargo scanned the terrain ahead for a way out of their predicament. The land was flat, but there was plenty of brush. Somehow, he must get Molly and Kevin to safety. Then he could tend to the Austrians.

They had gone half a mile when the duke cleared his throat. "You would make this easy on all of us, Kilmacthomas, if you would tell me where to find the emeralds. Then you can go your way in peace."

"You're a terrible liar, Metternick," Kevin said. "We both know you can't leave any of us alive."

"It's your brother's fault, not mine. He shouldn't have meddled in matters that didn't rightfully concern him. He's to blame for what will happen, if anyone is."

"William was a decent man, you bastard. Your government had no right killing him or his in-laws."

"No right!" Metternick exploded. "What do you know of rights, you drifting play-actor? Any sovereign government has the right to protect itself from rabble seeking to overthrow it, and those plotting to strip Austria of her power and territory are just that, common rabble!"

Riding ever westward, Fargo barely listened to their continuing argument. He racked his mind for a means of taking the Austrians unawares, but the two junior officers were spaced far enough out that should he try to ride one down, the other could immediately fire without fear of hitting the duke.

The Arkansas toothpick rested securely in his right boot. Somewhere along the line he must palm it and hide it under his sleeve until the proper time. The feeble moonlight would make the task easier.

Abruptly ahead there came a flicker of movement. Fargo peered into the brush and spied the bulky shape of a cow. Where there was one, there invariably were more. It must be more of the herd Miller owned. He glanced at the junior officers. Neither seemed to have seen the cow. They were both too intent on covering Molly, Kevin, and him.

He guessed their trail would take them within five to ten yards of where the cow stood. More materialized, all standing, apparently watching the riders approach. A desperate plan formed in his mind and he firmed his hold on the reins. Slim hope was all it offered, but he preferred it to certain death at the hands of the Austrians.

Soon they would be close enough. As yet, neither subordinate had glanced at the cows. He looked back at the duke, a shadowy figure at the end of the line, and spoke softly, as if worried he might be overheard. "Metternick, did you hear about the Cheyenne war party raiding these parts?"

"I did. What of it?"

"Warn your men. They're about to jump us," Fargo lied, hoping the duke hadn't heard about the fate of the war party from one of the acting company.

"What? How do you know? If this is some sort of trick—" Metternick began.

"Damn it, they're right there," Fargo said, and pointed at the herd of cattle.

The duke looked, saw the vague forms, and without taking time to think or study the shapes, he shouted to his men.

Which was exactly what Fargo wanted. "Follow me!" he yelled at Kevin and Molly, then reined hard to the right and rode straight at the cattle, whooping at the top of his lungs. Cattle were notoriously easy to spook. At night the hoot of an owl or the howl of a coyote might cause a herd to stampede. Predictably, these promptly scattered, running in all directions, many crashing into the brush and making enough noise to rouse a dead man.

Fargo was hoping all the commotion would momentarily confuse the Austrians. Unaccustomed as they were to western life, they would take a few seconds to figure out what was happening. By then he must have the others in the clear.

The Ovaro plunged into the stretch of brush, weaving among bushes, picking its way with the sure-footedness of a mountain lion. A shot blasted. He looked back, saw Molly and Kevin on his heels, and kept going. Another shot cracked, followed by angry words in German. The duke had guessed. Now the three Austrians would be after them in earnest.

He came out of the brush onto a flat expanse of snow and let Molly and Kevin come up on either side before goading the Ovaro into a gallop. If they could put distance between themselves and the pursuers, they'd lose them. He doubted the Austrians were capable of tracking in the dark.

Loud crashing in the brush signified the trio was in determined pursuit.

Fargo changed direction, riding north now. There was more shouting to their rear, and he gathered the Austrians were trying to figure out which way to go. The scattering cattle must have confused them.

On the spur of the moment he reined up. Molly and the Irishman did the same. They sat there silently in the dark, hearing their breathing and the cries of the Austrians.

"Did we lose them so soon, boyo?" Kevin whispered.

A bellow from the duke and the drumming of hoofs was his answer.

Lashing the reins, Fargo rode northward. The Ovaro could easily outrun the animals the Austrians were on, but his friends would be left behind. For the next mile they rode side by side. Then he turned yet again, bearing eastward.

As dark as it was, they were abreast of a draw before he spied it. "Keep going!" he urged the others, and slanted into the narrow draw, where he halted and wheeled the stallion. Holding the Ovaro perfectly still, he listened to the sounds of pursuit. Soon the Austrians pounded past, each gazing eastward, the duke leaning low to study the ground.

Fargo waited a few seconds, then up and out the draw he went. The Ovaro, having been through similar situations with him countless times before, knew what was expected and poured on the speed, flowing over the ground as if on air. He slipped his right boot free of the stirrup, drew his knee up, and managed to get the toothpick into his hand despite the rolling gait of the pinto.

The Austrians came into sight, still riding hard, still intent on overtaking their quarry.

Fargo gained ground steadily, the knife clutched in his right hand. If they saw him before he was close enough, they'd fill him full of lead before he could flee. Bending forward at the waist, his right arm hanging, he closed on the man in the rear, one of the junior officers.

From somewhere up ahead arose a shrill whinny and a scream of terror from Molly.

The Austrians heard. They slowed. And in that moment Fargo was on them, drawing alongside the last soldier. The man looked around and Fargo struck, sinking the knife into the man's neck and wrenching it loose as he streaked past. Too late, he realized the duke had turned his mount sideways. There was no time to stop.

Fargo hauled on the reins, turning the Ovaro just enough so that the big stallion struck the duke's smaller horse in the shoulder. The impact bowled the duke's mount over, and Fargo nearly lost his seat in the saddle. Tottering, the Ovaro almost fell, but retained its footing and leaped over the fallen horse in a smooth motion.

The collision gave the third Austrian an opportunity to close in, and as the Ovaro cleared the downed horse he rode up and extended his right arm, about to shoot.

Twisting, Skye saw the man coming. Evading the shot was impossible, so he did the next best thing. He did the totally unexpected. Instead of trying to run for it, he shoved clear of the Ovaro and leaped on the officer, swatting at the extended revolver as he did.

The gun boomed, the Austrian's eyes widened in surprise, and then Fargo seized the man by the front of his uniform and dropped, jerking the soldier off his horse. They landed on their sides, the Austrian retaining his grip on the gun.

Fargo stabbed at the man's gun arm, his knife slicing deep into the Austrian's shoulder. The soldier let go of his gun, roared in fury, and pulled his arm away. Blood flowed out and down his sleeve.

Scrambling erect, Fargo braced to attack again, keenly conscious of being vulnerable. The duke and the soldier he'd stabbed in the neck were somewhere nearby, perhaps training a gun on his spine. He must quickly dispose of this one so he could deal with the other two.

The officer was up, his right arm tucked to his body, his left fist balled and poised to strike. His eyes flicked past Fargo and he abruptly leaped to one side.

Skye heard the drum of thundering hoofs and imitated his adversary, but the horse was on him too rapidly. It felt as if a train had plowed into his back and he was hurled through the air to crash down with bone-wrenching force. Pain lanced his right arm. Stunned by the blow, he twisted and rose to his knees.

The Austrian with the neck wound was bearing down again, sitting the saddle unsteadily, a hand pressed over the wound.

Whipping his right arm up, Fargo was about to throw the toothpick, to try to pick the man off before that horse ran him down, when he realized he'd lost the knife when he'd been hit. Trying to find it in the dark would take precious time he didn't have. Crouching, he let the horse get closer, gauging its speed and distance critically. At the last instant before those flailing hoofs would have crushed him to the snow-covered turf, he darted to the right, reached up, and grabbed the rider's leg. His powerful shoulder muscles rippled as he lifted and pushed with all his might.

The Austrian, his arms flapping wildly, was thrown bodily from the saddle and fell onto his back.

Fargo reached the man in two bounds, delivering a right uppercut to the chin as the soldier attempted to stand. His knuckles snapped the man's mouth shut and dropped him flat, unconscious. Fargo started to turn so he could locate the duke and the other junior officer.

Steely arms looped around Skye from behind and he was lifted from the ground and shaken as a wolf might shake a small animal it had killed, his teeth chattering, his head rocking. Hot breath against his ear indicated where his attacker's face was positioned. Bending his head forward, he suddenly whipped it back.

There was a loud crunch, a startled oath in German, and the arms around Fargo let go. He landed lightly on the balls of his feet and whirled. The other subordinate stood a yard away, his nose pulped, blood streaming over his face and chin.

Growling like a wild beast, the Austrian moved forward, swinging his ponderous fists.

Fargo sidestepped the first punch, blocked the second, and rammed his right into the soldier's mouth. The man swayed on his heels but regained his footing and resumed slugging. A bruising punch clipped Fargo's cheek, splitting the skin. Another brushed his forehead as he ducked under it. The Austrian was good; he could box. But Fargo had done more than his share of brawling during his widespread travels. Through hard experience he'd learned how to handle himself, how to employ his fists to devastating effect, and he did so now, his muscular, whipcord body giving force to punches that staggered the Austrian.

Working under the handicap of having one arm already cut open, the soldier fought bravely, stubbornly, even when his lips had been reduced to a puffy mass and his right ear had been split wide.

Fargo fought in a cold, calculated fury. The same dilemma nagged at him. He couldn't afford to concentrate on this subordinate when the duke must still be alive and armed. He rained short jabs to the man's face, backing him up, and drove a straight arm into the soldier's midsection. Wheezing, the Austrian bent in half and Fargo kneed him full in the face. The man flipped onto the snow and lay still, groaning.

Hoofs thudded dully to Fargo's rear.

Pivoting, he saw a single horse approaching. On it were Kevin and Molly. He glanced around, saw that the duke's horse was back on its feet but there was no sign of the duke. The two junior officers were unconscious.

"We couldn't run out on you boyo," Kevin declared. "It wouldn't be right."

"You should have kept on going," Fargo chided them, scouring the vicinity for the duke.

"We didn't have much choice," Molly said. "My horse got its legs caught in a hole and went down, spilling me. I'm afraid its leg is broken."

"Ride off anyway!" Fargo directed. "Metternick is around here somewhere."

"I'm right here," announced the familiar stiff voice, and Duke Francis von Metternick walked around from behind Kevin's mount, a revolver firmly held in his right hand and tilted upward at the Irishman and Molly.

"Crawled out of your hole, did you?" Fargo taunted while desperately scanning the ground for anything he could use as a weapon.

"Don't be petty, Mr. Fargo," Metternick said sternly. "I've won, after all, as I knew I would. Have the decency to accept your defeat graciously.'"

About to make a rude retort, Fargo spied an object lying on the snow near the soldier he'd stabbed in the neck. The details were vague but the shape distinct. It was a gun!

"Now we will conclude this messy affair," the duke said, and raised his gun toward Kevin. "You will tell me where you have hidden the emeralds or I will kill the young lady."

"You miserable bastard!" Kevin retorted angrily.

Fargo didn't bother waiting for a better opportunity. There might not be one. He dived as if into a pool of water, his arms over his head, jarring his stomach when he landed a few inches shy of the revolver. A gun cracked and the snow near his face became a miniature geyser. He surged forward, his right hand closing on the butt, and rolled to the right.

The duke's gun barked again.

There was a stinging sensation as the bullet creased Fargo's shoulder, and then he had finished the roll and was staring up at Metternick. He thumbed the hammer and squeezed off a shot, and the duke, bored clear through in the act of taking aim, staggered backward.

Fargo rolled again and once more, and at the completion of each roll he squeezed off another shot. Each scored, smacking into Metternick's chest. With the third shot the duke's legs buckled and he sank to the ground, his gun falling from his slack fingers.

Duke Francis von Metternick, on his side with a dark stain spreading over his uniform, blinked at the big man in buckskins, blinked and said, "Congratulations, sir." Then he died.

The blast of the gun still ringing in Fargo's ears, he slowly stood. Fatigue washed over him and he wanted to lie down and sleep for a month. He was barely aware of Molly dismounting and coming over to him.

"Is it over?"

"Is it?" Fargo asked, glancing up at Kevin.

"It is as far as I'm concerned," the Irishman said. "My brother sent me the name and address of a man in Austria in his last letter. Said to get the emeralds to this man if the worst happened." He paused, his expression melancholy. "Bill should have married Maureen Flaherty back in Dublin."

Wearily Fargo draped an arm over Molly's slender shoulders. There were still a few things to do. The junior officers must be held for the marshal. The duke's body should be taken back to the Crossing. But Kevin and Miller could attend to those chores. Tired and bruised as he was, he had other priorities. Right now all he wanted was a soft bed under him and a willing woman at his side, and he already had the latter. He turned toward Miller's Crossing, smiling.

"What's so funny?" Molly asked, puzzled.

"You'll see," Fargo promised, and chuckled.

*Denver City, 1860,
where gold buys anything or anyone,
and greed can grind a man to dust.*

The six-horse team was losing ground, hooves scrambling in vain on the loose rocks of the steep trail leading out of the arroyo. The stagecoach driver cracked the whip over the horses' sweating backs and their eyes rolled in terror, lips drawn back, mouths foaming on the metal bits. The team struggled to find a foothold, but still they slipped backward down the slope, dragged by the stagecoach which tilted on three wheels and slid precariously toward the edge of the gulch.

As he mounted the crest of the rise, Skye Fargo's lake-blue eyes took in the scene at once—the trickle of water which had carved the hazardous ravine out of the high plain, the steep rocky path leading down into and up out of the gorge, the trail washed out and treacherous by a recent cloudburst, the lost wheel of the coach lying below the trail on the rocks, the team sliding toward the cliff and the dusty brown stagecoach, sure to follow. Fargo heard a woman's scream from inside the coach as it lurched backward a few more yards.

Fargo put the spur to the Ovaro and the muscular horse surged forward beneath him, moving surefootedly and fast down the trail into the ravine, splashing through the trickle of water and climbing up the steep bank, shortcutting the trail which was blocked by the coach. Fargo seized his lariat and leapt to the ground beside a *pinon* pine, knotting the sisal rope quickly around the rough bark of the twisted tree—an old one with deep roots, he thought gratefully.

Fargo dashed toward the horses and looped the rope around the crossbar between the lead ones. As he was hitching the rope the horses slipped again and the cord tightened across his fingers, catching two of them against the wooden crossbar. White pain flashed like sudden lightning. Fargo heard the awful sound of his own teeth grinding as he wrenched his fingers free of the tightening rope and it pulled taut.

One corner of the stagecoach already hung out in space over the gully. The door flew open. The passengers were panicking, Fargo thought. Any moment the ones closest to the door would make a jump for it, rocking the teetering coach and plunging it, along with the remaining passengers, over the edge of the cliff.

"Don't move!" he yelled above the whinnying of the team.

The sisal rope stretched, groaned once, then held. He would have to move fast. In an instant, Fargo eyed the heavy Concord coach—one ton of wooden joinery, iron, and leather. The team was jumpy. Any sudden movement would put an extra strain on the rope and it might snap, plunging the coach twenty feet down into the gulch. If one of the horses reared . . .

It wasn't over yet, Fargo thought as he strode toward the coach.

"Easy, easy," he calmed the team, touching the nearest ones on the necks and rumps as he made his way down the line. Now, if he could just keep the travelers calm and get them off the coach. There were two men on top, the driver and a grizzled prospector, by the look of his wide-brimmed hat.

"That was a close one," the greasy-haired driver said in a loud voice, wiping his face on his bandana. The stupid man seemed to think the coach was safe!

"Nobody move!" Fargo said.

He saw a woman's gloved hand grasp one side of the door jamb of the passenger door and a female voice—a young one— said, "Hell's bells! Best thing is if we can jump down out of this contraption!"

Then Fargo heard another sound, a sound he didn't like half so well—the low groan of the rope holding the stagecoach to the *pinon* pine.

"Don't move!" Fargo yelled again, coming up to the coach door. Through the window, he saw a face—a pert upturned nose and brown curls under a straw hat, and a pair of thick horn-rimmed glasses.

"Saints alive! We need to get down outta here!" she said.

Fargo saw the coach rock as the passengers inside moved about and he heard a crescendo of voices babbling like a brook after a snow melt.

The driver stood up on top of the coach and started to climb down. "Sure was a lucky thing . . ."

Lulled by their sudden relief, none of them was listening to him, Fargo realized. He'd have to act fast.

"Freeze!" said Fargo, drawing his Colt revolver and aiming it in the general direction of the descending driver. "Damn you, freeze!"

The driver and the old prospector both stiffened and slowly raised their hands. The voices inside came to an abrupt halt.

"Just my luck," the old prospector muttered. "We don't go over the cliff. But we get held up by a bandit."

"One word, one move, and you're dead," Fargo threatened. They would be dead, or at least badly injured if they continued to panic and the rope broke. There was silence. The horses shuffled.

"Do what I say and no one gets hurt," Fargo said, turning toward the passenger door. Out of the corner of his eye, he saw the driver easing his hands down under the seat, probably to fetch his rifle.

Fargo wheeled toward him.

"You, get down," Fargo commanded the driver. There was no time for women first. Besides, he needed help steadying the horses.

"Hands up," Fargo said. "Leave the rifle on board. Move slowly. Do exactly as I say. One false move and the coach goes over the cliff."

As the driver stepped off the running board onto the trail, the coach gave another jolt.

"You next," Fargo motioned to the old prospector. "Move slow."

The old man climbed down, more nimbly than the driver had and more quickly than Fargo would have expected.

Fargo holstered his Colt.

"Now that I have your attention," he said, "get to the front. Keep the team quiet." He saw the surprise and relief on their faces. "If the rope breaks, keep the horses steady. Without you two, the coach is lighter. The team should be able to keep it from sliding." He turned his attention to the passengers.

The pretty face in the window was all smiles. Fargo opened the door.

"Carefully, now. No sudden moves," he said, reaching up to lift her. He put his hands about her waist, a warm and rounded slenderness under a tight, fitted yellow bodice, which swelled and bloomed upward into high and fulsome breasts and downward into full hips under her blue riding skirt. Fargo lifted her easily and felt her wriggle slightly in his grasp. As he set her down, she removed her thick glasses and smiled. Her eyes were impossibly round and glossy brown, like her hair.

"Goodness gracious! Weren't we lucky you came along?" she said. Fargo smiled and turned back to the passenger door.

There in the doorway was a second girl, willowy and pale, as fragile as dawn, her long blond hair braided across her head and her eyes downcast. She was easing herself onto the running board, as if afraid to be helped.

"Allow me," Fargo said, reaching up to grasp her waist. She kept her eyes averted as he lifted her to the ground, noticing as he did that she was as weightless as a bird and she smelled of—he couldn't place it for a moment and then he had it—of lemons. Bracing. Fresh.

"Thank you very much," she said, smiling up at him shyly, then blushing and turning away.

Behind her, the last passenger, a graying man in a gray waistcoat, climbed carefully down from the coach.

"Paul Cavendish," he said advancing on Fargo and offering his right hand.

"In a minute," Fargo replied. "Let's get the coach hauled off this hair-raiser."

"Right," Cavendish agreed. "Tell me what to do."

"Brace the three wheels with rocks," Fargo said. "Wedge 'em in hard with a kick in case we start to slip." Cavendish did as he was ordered while Fargo hitched his Ovaro to the team.

When the wheels were braced, Fargo untied the lariat and quickly wound it, returning it to his saddle horn.

"You two get up the trail ahead of us," he commanded the two ladies, who quickly obeyed. "We don't want the coach rolling back over you if we lose it. You three men, go around to the back of the coach and hold up the rear end. I'll lead the team.

"Easy does it," he said softly to his Ovaro and to the horses, as he led them slowly up the rocky trail. Fargo kept the team moving slowly but steadily, until they gained the top of the ravine. He walked the team forward onto a flat section of the trail.

Fargo retrieved his lariat from the saddle. "I need one man to help me get the wheel," he said. The old prospector followed him down the trail, the loose gravel sliding under their boots as they descended.

The wheel lay on the steep slope below the trail, near the edge of the trickle of water.

"Wait here," Fargo directed him, handing him one end of the lariat. Fargo plunged down the slope, his muscular thighs catching his surfooted descent. He quickly knotted the rope through the spokes and ascended and the two of them hoisted the heavy wooden wheel up the rocky incline.

"There's your wheel," Fargo said, as he rolled it up over the top of the incline.

"Much obliged," the driver said. He had already fetched his toolbox.

"I'll help you," the prospector said. "I'm right handy with fixing." Together they bent to the task of fitting the wheel back onto the axle and replacing the main cotter pin which had jounced loose on the rough road.

Fargo unhitched his Ovaro from the team. He spotted a patch of tender shoots of bluegrass a short distance away. He led the pinto to the spot and put him on a long tether to graze.

Then the Trailsman straightened up to look around.

The high plains of eastern Colorado Territory rolled out in front of Fargo's eyes, with deep buffalo grass waving like ripples in a stream. The prairie was cut with deep gullies and dry canyons and gashed by dangerous ravines, like the one they had just come through.

This trail from Bent's Fort on the Arkansas River climbed steadily, and emerged onto the high plain called the Divide. It was not the Great Divide, which lay along the spine of the Rocky Mountains to the west. This Divide was the high plain between the valleys of the Arkansas River to the south and the Platte River to the north where Denver City lay.

At the coach, Cavendish was giving his arm to the willowy young woman, helping her out of the hot late afternoon sun. The driver and the old prospector bent over the wheel. The brunette had raised a parasol and was twirling it slowly on her shoulder, first one way and then the other, walking toward him. Her horn-rimmed glasses were folded and hung on a thin chain about her neck. As she walked, the spectacles bounced against the dramatic curves of her breasts, the chain catching on one and then the other swelling mound.

Fargo put one finger to the brim of his hat as she approached. She nodded and smiled.

"What a beautiful horse," she said.

The pinto nibbled contentedly, moving among the sweetferns and the tender blades of spring grasses pushing up through the sod. His fore and hindquarters gleamed black and the afternoon sun illuminated the startlingly white band across his midsection.

"I've never seen a horse with those markings. What kind is it?"

"Ovaro," Fargo said. "A kind of pinto."

"Looks strong," she said, but her eyes moved, not over the pony, but over his own broad chest and tall, muscular body. She smiled appreciatively, bewitchingly.

"Rompin' rescues!" she exclaimed, her brown eyes twinkling. "Did I thank you yet for saving us back there? My name's Pru," she said, extending her hand as a man would for a handshake. "Short for Prudence. Not that I have much of that my daddy always said."

She looked him full in the face, chin raised, watching his face for a reaction, her cheeks blushing a little.

Fargo laughed. She certainly wasted no time.

"Skye Fargo," he said, taking her hand, careful not to grasp it too hard.

"Pleasure," she replied. She removed her hand from his and began to stroke the Ovaro's neck with long, lazy motions.

"What's a pretty woman like you doing out in Colorado Territory?"

"I'm heading to Denver City," Pru said, continuing to rub the horse. "I'm from Baltimore, but it's such a bore. Jumpin' Jimmies, the men there all play tiddlywinks!"

Fargo felt her eyes on him again in unabashed appraisal of his lean body.

"There aren't any men like you back in Baltimore. If it hadn't been for you, we'd have toppled into that stream. We'd be dead, or hurt at least. I was really serious when I said we were lucky you came by. I—all of us—owe you a debt," she said and paused giving him a searching look. "How can we, I mean, I repay you?"

"No need to," Skye said, smiling down at her. She raised her eyebrows slightly and her eyes sparkled.

"Maybe if I think real hard, I might think of something mutually agreeable," she said, twirling her parasol.

"I don't like obligations," he said. "But mutual pleasure is something else again." She giggled and blushed.

"It's highly unusual to see a lady traveling alone," Skye said. "What are you planning to do in Denver City?"

"Well," she said slowly, as if collecting her thoughts. "One thing is to find a job. I've got a great head for figures. At least my daddy always told me that. I used to work for him in his bank. In fact," she added, her voice taking on a note of seriousness, "you remind me a lot of him. Daddy was a good man—the kind of man you could trust."

Fargo waited, saying nothing as she paused. She looked across the empty plains as if she saw a far-off thunderstorm. Her face darkened. "You see, I worked for him when he was the director of the First Bank of Baltimore."

"And then?" Fargo asked.

She spoke softly as if through a gray haze of memory. "There was the flu epidemic. Mother died and he just couldn't get over it. Then he sent me away so I wouldn't catch it. I didn't get home until he had died too."

Fargo saw the tears standing in her eyes.

"And then my brother, he was trying to be like my father. But the bank fired him. He never told me why, but it just crushed him. And then he went to . . ."

Pru stopped as she saw Cavendish approaching.

"That was a nice piece of rescue back there," Cavendish said as he walked toward them. "Allow me to introduce myself formally. Paul Cavendish." He extended his hand and shook Fargo's vigorously.

"Skye Fargo."

"Excuse me for interrupting," Cavendish said as he caught sight of Pru's face.

Pru excused herself hurriedly and walked back to the coach, wiping her eyes discreetly with her lace handkerchief.

"Do you know how much farther we travel today?" Cavendish asked.

"You can reach Seventeen-Mile House just about nightfall," Fargo said, referring to the next way station which was exactly seventeen miles from Colfax and Broadway in downtown Denver City. The network of stopovers, established by the stagecoach company, was named for the distance from the intersection of Denver City's two main streets. The stations spread out in a gigantic web on all the trails that led to the city and offered fresh horses and mules, water, fodder, and sometimes a hot meal and a place to sleep.

"What's the trail like from here on in?" Cavendish asked.

"Now that you've gained the Divide, it will be an easy time of it. All the way to Denver City. If the Indians cooperate."

Denver City. He felt the pull of it. Fargo caressed images of leisurely hot baths with some good strong soap, some frilly female company, a couple of fancy meals, and maybe a few sharp and fast card games—a whole week of rest and relaxation, much needed after his last arduous trail.

"You heading to Denver City?" Cavendish asked him.

"Planning to," Fargo said.

Fargo turned and took the measure of Paul Cavendish—his neatly clipped graying beard and the smart gray waistcoat, gold watch fob looped across his chest, and shiny black boots. Cavendish's face was lined with concern, as if he carried a great weight on his shoulders. His gray eyes were steady, penetrating.

"This your first time in Colorado Territory?" Fargo asked.

"No," Cavendish said. "I'm from Boston originally. But I moved out to Denver City six months ago. I was just back east to bring my daughter Laurel to live with me. She's attended a girls' school in Boston since her mother died four years ago."

"Pretty girl," Fargo said with a nod toward the coach, where the two women sat with the doors open to catch the afternoon breeze. "What are you doing in Denver City?"

"That was a nasty gulch," Canvendish said, changing the subject. "To look at this plain, you wouldn't expect these sudden ravines."

"Water run off," Fargo said, wondering what Cavendish was hiding. "There's not enough ground cover to stop the snowmelt or the sudden spring showers, once the water gets going. This country's famous for flash floods."

"This is the first time I've been on this trail," Cavendish admitted. "I've gone back and forth a few times to Philadelphia, but always before I've traveled through Leavenworth, Kansas."

"That's the direct route from the east," Fargo said. "Why are you taking the long way around?"

"Just curious about the trail," Cavendish said, evasive again.

Fargo glanced over and saw that the wheel was replaced on the stagecoach. The old prospector was handing the tools up to the driver who was storing them in the box under his seat.

Fargo untied his horse, and he and Cavendish walked toward the coach. The prospector straightened up at their approach.

"Mighty obliged to you," he said to Fargo, extending a rough hand. "Sweeteye Sam's the name. Didn't catch yours."

"Fargo. Skye Fargo."

"Climb aboard," he said.

Pru placed a slender foot into the stirrup and Fargo caught a glimpse of lacy garters and shapely legs as she swung up onto the horse.

Then he swung up into the saddle behind her and clucked to

the Ovaro. They moved slowly out in front of the coach, Fargo's muscular arms around Pru, holding the reins.

With every gentle sway of the horse Pru seemed to relax and melt against Fargo's broad chest. Even her back and shoulders felt soft, giving, like a cloud of cotton, and her hair was warm and woman-scented. Words seemed to be unnecessary as they rode through the gradually darkening plain. Fargo was enjoying the closeness of Pru, her softness, her sweet smell, the sight of her tantalizingly curved breasts as he looked down over her shoulder. It had been a long trail and he was tired out, ready for anything that was not cold, dangerous, or uncomfortable. At least for a while.

After a few miles, in the distance she spotted a long low line of trees along one of the gulches.

"What kind of trees are those?" Pru asked. She raised her arm and pointed—unnecessarily—and leaned against his left arm. He felt the warm full softness of her left breast press against his hard bicep. She remained there, her firm breast rubbing up and down gently with the gait of the horse.

"Cottonwoods," he said, bringing his mouth close to whisper it into her ear.

He felt himself harden against the gently swaying warmth of her pressing up against him in the saddle. He felt himself swelling with desire, wanting her. She felt it too and shifted her rounded hips against him.

"Knocking nightshirts, Skye," she said, turning half around in the saddle, to catch his eye. "I'll bet you don't even know what tiddlywinks are!"

Fargo laughed and tightened his arms around her as she nestled into his chest. He watched her horn-rimmed glasses bouncing against her breasts.

Later, he promised himself silently. Later tonight.

RIDING THE WESTERN TRAIL

- [ ] THE TRAILSMAN #99: CAMP SAINT LUCIFER by Jon Sharpe. (164431—$3.50)
- [ ] THE TRAILSMAN #100: RIVERBOAT GOLD by Jon Sharpe. (164814—$3.95)
- [ ] THE TRAILSMAN #101: SHOSHONI SPIRITS by Jon Sharpe. (165489—$3.50)
- [ ] THE TRAILSMAN #103: SECRET SIXGUNS by Jon Sharpe. (166116—$3.50)
- [ ] THE TRAILSMAN #104: COMANCHE CROSSING by Jon Sharpe. (167058—$3.50)
- [ ] THE TRAILSMAN #105: BLACK HILLS BLOOD by Jon Sharpe. (167260—$3.50)
- [ ] THE TRAILSMAN #106: SIERRA SHOOT-OUT by Jon Sharpe. (167465—$3.50)
- [ ] THE TRAILSMAN #107: GUNSMOKE GULCH by Jon Sharpe. (168038—$3.50)
- [ ] THE TRAILSMAN #108: PAWNEE BARGAIN by Jon Sharpe. (168577—$3.50)
- [ ] THE TRAILSMAN #109: LONE STAR LIGHTNING by Jon Sharpe. (168801—$3.50)
- [ ] THE TRAILSMAN #110: COUNTERFEIT CARGO by Jon Sharpe. (168941—$3.50)
- [ ] THE TRAILSMAN #111: BLOOD CANYON by Jon Sharpe. (169204—$3.50)
- [ ] THE TRAILSMAN #112: THE DOOMSDAY WAGONS by Jon Sharpe.
  (169425—$3.50)